WORDS

LOVE CAN BE DEVASTATING

A DARK MYSTERY NOVEL BY

MILLIE SCHMIDT

Written by: Millie Schmidt
Edited by: Schmidt Millie
English Language Counseling by: Liberty Fitz-Claridge
Cover Photograph by: Michelle Yug
Book and Cover Design: Sparrow Publishing
Published by: Sparrow Publishing

SPARROW
PUBLISHING YOUR KNOWLEDGE

For those interested in writing to Millie Schmidt:
E-mail: millenium2124@gmail.com

BEWARE!

What you are about to read is based on a true story, which took place in the belly of the city of Tel Aviv, on the coast of the Mediterranean Sea, and in worlds adjacent to it.

All people and creatures depicted in this book are used fictitiously, and names and certain details have been changed to protect the privacy of those involved. There was no ill intent in the retelling of this story, and no desire to harm those involved, beyond the harm that's already been done to them.

Oh, and don't be scared.
These are just... words on paper.

You have been warned.

"He who fights with Monsters should look to it that he himself does not become a Monster. And when you gaze long into the Abyss, the Abyss also gazes into you."

Friedrich Nietzsche, Beyond Good and Evil

CONTENTS

THIS IS NOT
A LOVE STORY

CHAPTER I

SHE WAS DOOMED

She was doomed the moment she walked in.

The room was so small she couldn't even open the window all the way. The whole place was very narrow, and a big mirror covered the wall to her left. She looked at herself for a moment, in the white neon light. Her curly hair looked dark, almost brown, and her cheeks were red. She was wearing only a blue shirt that lay tight against her young breastsW, and a pair of shorts. Nothing fitting for the upcoming winter. But that's all she came with, and she couldn't go back for more.

Her brown eyes looked at our reflection in the mirror.

"I told you it's small." We said.

"Yeah." She chuckled and turned around to us. "But it's okay."

"You can sleep here tonight, and just leave tomorrow."

She smiled. "What are you gonna do tomorrow?"

"Write. As usual."

Since she was underage, let's just call her **Y**.

We've met not long ago, like we've met many girls who came and went away. That's life... And that night we looked at her sitting on the bed. It was low and narrow, barely fitting for two people, but when we told her that would be the case, **Y** said it's okay.

She came of her own free will. Believe us, that's also why she stayed.

"How long have you been here?" She said.

"A month, maybe. I don't keep time."

We told her that the bed doesn't fit for two. She knew it will be crowded.

"It's really cool that you have a place of your own, and you can just write all the time."

"Well," We said. "That's the point."

"What is?" She said.

"The search of Inspiration."

"Tell me about it!"

Now we looked at the mirror, and the deep dark eyes looked right back. It's been a month or so, but we were actually in the city for about three. For the past two months we were sleeping on a sofa at a... friend's apartment. We needed money for a place of our own, and we needed a job. That's when Moon came in.

"Why are you here?" We said.

"You said I can sleep here." Said Y.

"Yeah, I mean... why are you in Tel Aviv?"

Most young people in this city were not born in it. Y and us, we are no exception. So for every person you've met you could always ask why, and get a story. We've met Y once and for five minutes, so we didn't have much time to talk about it.

Then she came to us.

"I... just don't wanna be at my parents' house too much." Said Y. "We don't really get along."

"So where do you usually sleep?"

"At a friend's."

Well, seemed like we were friends. For us, she could have been a source of Inspiration. Just like Moon and the rest of them.

"My parents and I don't agree on many things."

"The usual." We said. "How old are you? Sixteen?"

"Fourteen." Said Y.

She was a clean slate. However, not something to rely on. It should have ended that night.

Y got up from the bed and touched her shirt, and her breasts swayed. She had pale, smooth skin and big lips, and a short neck leading to her breasts. Her waist was a little wide, and the blue of her fingernails was peeling.

"Can I go take a shower?" Said Y.

"Sure." We said. "You don't have to ask."

"I always ask."

"You're sleeping here tonight." We said. "Feel free."

The shower and the toilet were hidden behind a drywall. There was no door, only a curtain that smelled of damp water. All we needed was a place to write all this, no matter how awful it was. We were, in a way, quite desperate.

The big black cockroach looked straight at us.

We killed him.

The place was full of them. For the past month, every night we lay in bed, and in the dark we could hear the scratches in the walls. Every night we would turn on the light to see one or two, as long as our middle finger and thick. Every night we killed.

Every night we wrote about the passing day. Our goal in coming here was to find something to write about, in order to become an author. Well, sort of. It wasn't the only goal, but it's the only one you should know about for now.

When we were Y's age our life was wasted. Now we had to fix everything.

"I'm done." Said Y. Her hair was smooth and heavy of water, and her breasts were hidden under a small yellow towel. Her shoulders were bear.

"Wear this." We handed her the bathrobe that was hanging next to the bed. Our bathrobe.

We turned around until she was finished. The bathrobe was of a hue between red and brown and it looked disgusting, but that's all we had. Then Y closed her eyes while we went in the shower.

There was a catch, though.

When they built this room, they put the toilet right in front of the opening in the drywall. Behind the drywall was the shower, and you had to step over the toilet seat to get in. Luckily for you, you weren't there.

We already had a hard-on as we thought of her there, outside. She was the first one to see this horrible place. Even we weren't there most of the time, but when Y said she needed a place to sleep for one night, we invited her. We couldn't leave her on the street, and we also wanted to see what she can do.

Girls were Inspiration.

We never had inspiration, and we realized at one point that we have to live in order to write. And when we write, time freezes. A world is born. And we are King.

The water turned cold and we told her we were coming out. Y was waiting for us to get dressed before she opened her eyes. She smiled.

11

We turned off the neon lights and turned on the nightlight. The little cell was filled with yellow fingers of light crawling on the walls, and we sat next to Y on the bed. It was the only place we could sit on, except for a hard, wooden chair that stood beneath the window.

"Aren't you gonna write?" She said.

"I wrote this whole day before I went out to get you."

She lay down beside us and we looked at her. Her eyes were very warm, and the yellow light reflected from them.

"You could have just explained where the apartment is..." Said Y.

"I'm not blaming you." We smiled. "I'm just saying I'm done for today. And it's not an apartment..."

"Can I see what you wrote?"

"No."

Y chuckled in our bed. "Do you have a lot of secrets?"

"Yes." We said.

"When can I know them?" She said.

Hope you never will.

We turned off the light and the cell was drenched in darkness. The window was shut and the air was still. The wind was roaring in the bushes outside, but there was no other sound. No cars, no neighbors, no laughter.

And just before we fell into a world of dreams and nightmares, we felt something crawling on our skin.

It was too dark to see the ceiling, and we were too low to see the mirror. Y's fingers were caressing us, going down between our legs. We were hard.

We were hard anyway. Only now it was harder.

She was too young for us.

But our hands moved inside the bathrobe and on her round breasts. Our fingers found her nipples, and she let out a sigh. It was dark and we could barely see her, but we could feel her warm breaths on our neck and her fingernails on our cock. We lay on top of her and opened the bathrobe, and our lips began sucking at her nipples. Y moaned harder.

Any word we might say could stop this.

We didn't say a thing.

We went on and on, and all of our hands were busy. Until eventually, Y went down between our legs and put our cock in her hot, wet, mouth, and sucked it. Our hands went through her curls. Her hands were on our waist. We felt her tongue and teeth, and we began breathing hard.

Nothing else existed outside of this black narrow cell. There was nothing but her mouth and our cock. And when we couldn't take it anymore we thrust deeper and we came, and Y coughed a little in the dark. Her shady figure rose from our crotch and she swallowed it all.

She was too good for us.

And when she came back to lie next to us we hugged. We were both tired enough anyway, and it was time to leave this world. Our thoughts began dispersing and becoming incoherent. We weren't just older than her... We were thousands of years old.

But before we go on, there's something else. Two months of wandering through this city, looking for a job and Inspiration. We should tell you more about how we got in that cell, about Y and Moon, and about how it all started.

13

Well, not all.

After all, we do have many secrets.

If **Y** will read this somewhere, someday, she'll know at least some of them.

You'll know too, if you continue.

CHAPTER II

~

THE HOTEL

You can't find a bigger city in this country than Tel Aviv, and you can find anything you want in it. We arrived in autumn in search of Inspiration. Our small town had nothing, and we wasted our most valuable years sitting at home. But writers need to live.

There's only one way to shape the world and it's through written language. Those who master this art can conquer time and space. But we're not supposed to talk about that so early in our story.

The important thing was the tall buildings shining in the sun, the beach at the end of the street and all those people from all over the country. We met Moon when we came to spend a day in the big city. She already lived there. Moon was friends with some people we knew, but when they left to go home, we stayed there with her. We were lying on the grass that evening, behind the big and empty school.

Moon was a bit fat and she wore silver rimmed glasses. Her hair was light brown and flowed around her round face, ending between her shoulder blades. All of our friends were already gone that night, but we stayed and talked to her until our lips touched and hands started searching for soft spots.

Moon wasn't really into talking. And we knew, of course, we weren't anything special for her. There were others before us, and there will be others in the future. But that night we were there, and our fingers were inside her as she sighed and moaned. And when she had enough she rubbed our cock until we came on the grass. We were lying on our sides, looking at the white fluid dripping from the leaves towards the ground.

That's how we became friends.

At least for a short time.

When we arrived in Tel Aviv again, this time to stay, we knew Moon is the one to talk to.

While waiting to hear from her, we took a walk around the city. It was sunny and the people were rushing in their daily routines. Nobody noticed us. You could see all kinds of people, if you were there. But then again, luckily, you weren't.

The streets were going in all directions, one to the beach, one to the market, one to the mall... Leaning against the wall was a homeless man with his bare leg in front of him, full of open wounds. They were round and shallow and filled with thick red...

And that's when Moon texted us.

"You should get down here. They look for workers in my hotel."

She also gave an address, so we had no choice but to go. We wanted to start a new life, away from the past. Towards... well, future plans are what we can't discuss yet.

It was all a part of the mission. If we want to find good stories, we have to say "yes" to this place, no matter what it may bring. Our mission is to gather as much as possible from this world, in order to create another one.

You cannot attain eternity, without seizing a few moments.

And so we went through the crowded market to the hotel. It was very narrow and very dirty, and the road was stained with puddles of dark water. There were fruit skins and nylon bags and old, wrinkled people, like we'll never be. The street vendors were shouting and pointing at their goods, and none of it looked appealing. Cats were walking between the stalls in hope of getting something to eat, and flies were buzzing in the air and in our ears.

It was a jungle in broad daylight.

We went from alley to alley, stepping over the sewage waters and the full trash bags half open, with their contents spilling on the ground.

Then we were out and saw the big hotels not too far from the shore. A wide patch of grass separated them from the water. The weather was clear and the buildings were high and shining white in the sun, all their windows glittering.

Moon said to come around the back, but she wasn't there when we arrived. Instead, there stood a tanned man with a straight nose and black eyes, looking straight at us.

"Moon is working. She said she'll be here soon." He said and took one hand out of his pocket. We shook it. "I'm in charge of the dining hall workers. Moon said you're looking for a job."

"I am." We said.

He scanned us with his eyes. There was no wind, and there was no one else there. It was just us, and him.

"Is that the office?" We said.

"Um... for now. We don't need an office for that." Said Mr. In-Charge. "We need someone to come here and clear the dishes off the tables in the mornings. Sometimes you can work in the hall in the evenings... it's really not that hard."

"Okay." We shrugged.

"Do you intend to leave somewhere in the near future?"

Hopefully.

"No." We said.

"Okay." He turned around to his car and handed us a form. "Can you start now?"

What a nuisance. So this is the world of all those people, who mind their business in the dark. We have to participate. And since we had nothing better to do, we said "yes".

"Good. So you can change inside, and I'm sure Moon will be happy to teach you everything." He smiled. "But fill out the form, please."

We handed the form after five minutes and entered a small, humid, back room. To our sides were big laundry carts full of black and white uniforms, and their rubber wheels left black stripes on the floor. A tall guy nodded towards us as he pushed one of the carts outside.

"You should wear these." Said Moon.

She came in from the corridor at the other end of the room. Her hair was gathered and she looked good in her buttoned, white shirt, and black apron. We thought of our last meeting as she waved at Mr. In-Charge, grabbed us by the hand and pulled us in.

"We're almost done so you won't do much today." She said. "But you can watch and learn."

Moon handed us a pair of black pants, a black apron and a buttoned white shirt.

"These are yours. You can change in the toilet."

She waited outside as we changed, and all we could think of was that evening on the grass. We never lie, as far as you know, and although the job was far from what we wanted, we stayed because of Moon. She was our way out. And it was better being with her, than sitting in some shop and watching the cars pass by outside.

Moon just led us through the corridor with her fast paced walking. We walked a step or two behind her. She was young, her skin was immaculate, her hair smooth. She would fit very well in some sort of ritual, lying down on a stone surface, her hands are tied...

"They really need people." She said. "That's why we're here. The work is not too bad, and the boss is really nice. He's in charge, you know, if you ever need anything."

"So it wasn't your first choice either?" We said.

"It was the only place that agreed to hire me." She looked at us. "Still, I'm only seventeen."

"I had no idea."

"Now you shut up and listen. The dining hall serves breakfast every day, and we're the ones setting the tables in the morning and taking away the dishes when people are done."

"Do we wash the dishes?"

Moon puffed with closed lips. "Hell no. there's an automatic dishwasher. You just give the dishes to the workers and they put them in the machine."

"It sounds... disgusting." We looked at her.

"What is?" Said Moon.

"I hate leftovers."

"What other options do you have?"

"None." We said.

We could give up and leave the city, but then again we couldn't. Even when we wanted to, late at night, in bed, peering at the darkness. Once we've made a decision we had to stick to it, even if we didn't know why. We could argue with ourselves, but it was pointless. We had to go on with this. We had to take part in their world, in order to build ours.

An elevator took us up, and as we stood there we couldn't help but looking at her. It's been two months maybe, since we last saw her on the grass.

"And don't use your phone during shifts." Said Moon. "Fat Man doesn't like it."

"Who's he?"

"There are two shift managers. Fat Man and Little Boy."

The elevator doors opened.

"What's that?" Said the fat man who stood there in a too tight suit. He had a thick moustache and a stern look, which he shot straight at us.

"That's the new guy. I'll show him everything." Said Moon.

"You're both done in fifteen minutes!" Said Fat Man and disappeared.

"Look." Moon grabbed our hand again.

Her palm was warm and moist, and sent a tingling sensation down our spine. That was the hand that grabbed our cock back then. We peered into the dining hall, which was almost empty. Behind all the tables were glass sliding doors and through them we could see the Mediterranean Sea.

There was this guy there, loading a wide, round tray with plates and cups. His straw colored hair was gathered on his the back of his neck. He crouched, put one shoulder under the round tray, and straightened himself. The tray sat balanced on his shoulder and hand as he walked towards us in big steps, passed in front of us and put the tray on the metal surface of the dishwashing machine. He started unloading the tray when a black man, dressed in a yellow shirt, waved his hand at him, telling him to leave it. The waiter got back to work while the other guy started putting the dishes in the machine.

The noise was crackling fire.

"I'm going to have to do this?" We said.

"What? Loading the tray?" Said Moon. "You can clear the plates with your hands, but it'll take you hours. You need to work fast around here."

"I can't lift such a thing."

"You'll learn." She said. "Everybody learns. It's not like you have to be a superhuman..."

We begged to differ, but remained silent.

"You just take the plates and give them to these guys, and they take care of it." Said Moon. "Don't do any more work than you have to. We're not getting paid enough for that." She stood in front of us, and we could grab her... "In the morning you do the opposite. You take the clean plates and set the tables."

"Show me tomorrow, then."

"I'll show you now. I don't know if I'll be here tomorrow." She went over to the metal surface and started arranging some of the dishes. "One plate. Fold a napkin and put it on the right side, and then put the cutlery on it. It has to be on the napkin, not on the table. Put the fork to the left and the knife to the right. To the left of the plate you put this cup on this saucer. Put the cup upside down, of course." Moon demonstrated everything as she talked. "The handle must face away from the plate, and so does the spoon handle, which you place here." She put a spoon on the saucer.

"And you need a placemat under all that." Said a girl who passed behind us.

"Yeah, yeah." Said Moon. "And a table cloth. You'll see."

"Moon!" We heard the shout.

We turned around to see Fat Man standing there. His tie was crooked. So was his moustache.

"Why are you still here?!" He shouted.

"I'm showing the new guy..."

"Never mind that! Come back tomorrow noon!" Said Fat Man and pointed at us. "You, come in the morning! That's how you learn!"

This guy would make a great character. And once we write him, he's like that forever: his hair turning grey, his face square and red, shouting, moustache, small black eyes, a suit and a crooked tie, and his height. Fat Man was at least two heads taller than us.

Moon was a head shorter. She looked at us on our way down.

"Well, seems like you're on your own tomorrow." She said.

CHAPTER III

~

FULL MOON

It was dark outside and the stars were pairs of eyes in the purple sky. The treetops were still and the trunks were monster fingers. The sea was endless black water, and Moon was out with her friends for her eighteenth birthday.

We were working for about two weeks and we haven't seen her much. We didn't work every day and neither did she. The others taught us all the rest, and lifting the heavy, round tray was becoming an instinct. The dining hall in the mornings was quiet, and the sea was shining bright.

That night we were looking for her.

We spent most of the afternoons at the bookstore in the mall. There were big tables there where you could read or write, and we carried our notebooks with us to write there. Notebooks were easier to carry, but most of all, they were more efficient. Not only there was no internet, mind you, but there was also something else.

There was ink on paper.

Our papers were blank at first, but by scratching them as if to draw blood, we could change everything.

That night, Moon was in her favorite sushi restaurant, not far from our hotel. It was small, hidden beneath a leaning tree. It blocked the stars from view. The place was crowded, and the bartender nodded at us. We nodded back. Moon was in the back, and we went to see her.

"Oh, you came!" She said.

Her body was warm.

"Where is everyone?" We said.

"Gone already. You're late." Said Moon. "Sit down."

We sat on the corner sofa. She was in one side of the table, and we were on the other side. The table itself was a little square, and it looked dark in the orange light of the place. She was still eating what was left of her sushi.

"Happy birthday." We said.

"It's only next week." Moon shrugged. "Now's just the preparation."

"What do you need to prepare?"

She looked up at the lamp. "Nothing special, really. You can come too."

"When is it?"

"Next weekend." Said Moon while eating. "Not this one. Eat something."

We ate some just so that she won't have to throw it away. But while we did, we felt her legs on ours.

Now, pay attention. Moon was seventeen, but not naïve. She knew what she wants and she's gotten it a thousand times. We didn't have to ask to know this.

In one of the few days we worked together we got out of the hotel, and she said: "I like you. We're similar."

"How?" We said.

"You'll do anything for sex."

And that was all we needed to know. You see, she was mistaken about us. But in that one sentence she gave us all of her.

When you give, we take.

And so after complaining about work and about her roommate, and after finishing the saké, we started again. Moon's hands were all over us, she didn't care, and our mouths were full of saliva.

"We should get out." She Said.

She paid for everything and we got out to the street. It was as orange as the light inside the little restaurant, and the road was empty, and everything was silent but the echoing sound of children laughing.

She was walking away, and we hurried after her. Moon turned around.

"My roommate's home." She said.

We closed the gap between us and got back to kissing her and touching her breasts, and she leaned back on a parking car. It was a black station wagon on a small driveway. On the other side of it was a wall, and behind it was a basketball court.

"We can stay here." We said but didn't know why.

Moon's eyes looked as if she's about to object, but her lips didn't move. We moved her hair from her face and kissed her again. Her hands were gripping us, and we started moving away from the street towards the back of the vehicle. A single lamplight cast an orange ellipse that we slowly moved out of, into the shadows behind the station wagon. We collapsed on the tar surface.

There were kids in the basketball court.

It was surrounded by a tall fence from all sides, and they were on the other side of the court. They were probably Moon's age.

But she was too busy to notice, as she opened our pants and started rubbing our cock again.

"I have condoms in my bag." She said.

We let her do it all, just to get this over with. Moon was one of the only people we knew in this city, she was safety. And that night she was a pale, ghostly figure straddling us on the dirty floor, and we had no care in the world.

We lifted her shirt and held and sucked her breasts. They were big and pale, and her nipples were hard between our fingers. The kids were bouncing the ball in the court, and the sound was echoing from the car and the buildings. It was one moment, a rather short moment, that could become eternity. And as we came, so it was.

No one knew we were there.

And as Moon left and went home, we passed through the smaller streets and alleys, and the wind was warm. Wind filled us with air and made us feel as if we're high above the Earth.

The stars were looking back at us, and as we were walking we couldn't help but feel that there's somebody there. Someone was always walking with us.

We were writing and writing until our little finger was covered with black ink from the pages. It was the mark of the trade. We wrote everything we knew about Moon, her appearance, her character, and how she suddenly appeared and vanished over and over again. The hour got late, but it didn't matter. It was better than staring at the dark and answering the voices in your head.

The next time we saw Moon was the weekend. It was one weekend before her birthday, and we were working the night shift in the hotel. We liked being so high above the street, looking at the stars and the sea. It was dinner time for the hotel guests, but at the evenings the dining hall was usually emptier than in the mornings. And since it was Friday, people went out for restaurants in the city.

So we just did whatever Fat Man or Little Boy told us to do, which usually was to go and help in the hall, where people came to celebrate or get married. This Friday it was Fat Man's turn, and he was shouting through his stubby neck.

We finished and got out to the street. Moon didn't have many friends in the hotel, and so did we. In that manner, we were similar.

She complained about her roommate again as we walked. That Friday the house was empty, and we were on our way there. It wasn't too far from the hotel, further into the city and away from the sea. We were still exploring the city, and in our free time we walked around with our notebook. Tel Aviv was bigger than we thought and we couldn't cover all of it, but the area around the hotel was becoming more and more familiar.

It was not enough.

Working there was an adventure in and of itself, however, we also knew we have to search beyond the borders of the hotel. Search for... you will know in the end. We came to this city for this search, for this mission. Please, do not forget this.

And as we looked at Moon, who was talking about her parents, we knew her part was almost over.

We could get rid of her.

But we could fuck her again before that.

And as she let us in her dark apartment, we walked behind her to her room door. We went in and she turned the lights on. It was a mess. A part of the glass panel in the door was missing. Her desk

27

was full of books and papers, and there were empty beer bottles near the wall.

"You drink a lot." We said.

"It helps me pass the time." Said Moon.

"You're not even eighteen."

"Ever heard of a fake ID?"

The bed was large and took most of the space in the room. The window was closed. We could do whatever we pleased.

We looked at the glass panel in the door.

"I threw a shoe through it." She said. "My roommate's pissing me off."

We were naked in no time. There was no time to waste. Now Moon was lying on her back and we were on top, and inside her. She moaned and bit her lip and closed her eyes behind her glasses. This was all that she wanted.

We weren't similar at all.

And still, we buried our face in her fat breasts and pushed deeper and deeper, until we couldn't take it anymore and flowed inside of her. Moon let out a squeal as we collapsed upon her, searched her lips and kissed her hard.

Moon touched her lower lip with her finger and looked at its tip.

"I'm bleeding."

She was.

Our eyes met hers and held them in place, and she swallowed.

"It's a bite wound." Said Moon.

"It's okay." We said.

We were tired, and we could have stayed inside of her and take the blood away from her lip. But Moon preferred to get up and wipe it, and left us sitting on the bed.

"Why are you so sad?" She looked at us.

"What?"

"You're staring." Said Moon. "Every time you come you have this sad look in your eyes."

"It's... nothing special." We got up.

"Okay. Get dressed."

We did.

We went out to find the toilet. The house was rather small and very messy, and the only lights were those of the streetlamps pouring in from outside.

As we listened to the sound of piss hitting the water, it was mixing with the wind blowing outside. It was a strange night.

We went back down the dark path to her room, and opened the door. Moon closed her closet doors and looked at us. Her teeth were sharp and her hair messy and her eyes were pure white. Blank pages.

She hissed.

We got out and left the house, and we never saw her again. Our legs kept on walking as far as we could. We walked and walked. Things lost their physicality in the trance of walking. We could cross great distances without ever feeling it. Like there is no Body walking. Just us.

As for Moon, you'd think there was more to it, but there wasn't. Believe us. Moon was an angry child who only wanted to get fucked, and if it wasn't us it would have been someone else. We've known each other for a very short time, and it was enough to give us what we needed. We kept her here in these pages, so that her story will never end.

She is now our living exhibition.

We found ourselves at the foot of a wooden flight of stairs. The sign said, The Blue Bar. We climbed inside, passed the restroom and entered a crowded room full of strangers. But they had bodies.

A chubby singer with curly hair was singing on stage.

"What can I get you?" Said the tall, blond guy behind the bar.

"Whiskey. No ice."

The singer was almost screaming as he strummed his guitar.

"Oh, he's a regular." Said Blondy. "You'll get to know all of them if you'll come often enough. That's your first time here."

"Are you here every day?"

"I'm the owner." He said. "So basically, yeah."

It was a warm place and the walls were covered with all kinds of stickers and writings. After two glasses of whiskey we had to pee, and so we made our way to the toilet. A bald guy came out and we entered, and listened to the sound of piss mixing with the music. The walls were red and covered with writings, and to our right, something seemed to vibrate.

On the wall was a black inscription, and it seemed like the square letters were thickening and thinning over and over again. Like a beating heart.

Look for no. 14. N.

We looked at the ceiling and saw swear words, phone numbers, or song lyrics. If this was a dream constructed by our mind, the writings would change once we look at them again. It's called a reality check. They have to change, because they're not really there.

Look for no. 14. N.

Well, it must have been a very weird dream, then. We realized we were done peeing a long time ago, so we got out. The music also stopped. When we looked inside the main room from the toilet, the lights were flickering. There were still bodies there, sitting.

We stood in the doorway.

Then Blondy turned his head towards us.

He looked sick and tired.

The lights went on and off.

Look for no. 14. N.

We decided to quit. When you dive inside it for too long, dealing with words and Death and all that, things become a bit... strange. We counted our fingers to make sure we're awake.

When you dream it's your mind that creates the world, and if you manage to confuse it and find the anomalies, you know it's a dream. You can do so with the little things: like counting your fingers, trying to read or tell time, or by looking in the mirror.

You should never look in the mirror in your dreams.

This is called a reality check. We know this, and now you know this.

We had five fingers that night. We were awake.

This seemed real.

And that's how we began our descent into the belly of this city.

Come with us.

Don't be scared.

CHAPTER IV

AND SO IT BEGAN

You can't write without madness, and by that we mean possession. This means offering your mind and body to the influence of great spirits. We knew it can be done, because it happened over and over again in the past, and we knew this is the way now. Forget anything they've told you. Possession is real.

Possession means that we have to give up all our limitations and be open to Inspiration, of books, of music, of women, of nights. Of a new life. And lowering your guard is done best through drinking.

The stories you know deal with humans, however this one is a story of strange creatures walking the Earth. The streets, actually.

Arthur Rimbaud once said, "I is another."

And so we had to become another.

"Get dressed. We need to go." Said Y.

"We can be naked before we go." We said.

Y laughed. "No, let's go meet Lucas. They're waiting."

It feels like we've told this story an infinite number of times. Maybe because it repeated itself all throughout history, with all of the people who expanded their world and perception by traveling, by drinking, by fucking, by writing. We did it all, believe us.

Last night, the darkness was feathers on our skin.

The rain was washing the streets outside as we lay in bed, listening to her breaths. Y was calm for no good reason. She's known us for about a month now and she didn't know us at all. Well, we didn't really let her. But at nights we could caress her hair and cheeks and stare at the darkness. Whenever we closed our eyes they hurt, as we were forcing them to shut. We had to open them. There were many things in the room. There are many things all the time. We see and hear them.

Words came to us almost like magic. Someone else was reciting them. Word after word came to the front stage, to the light, creating forms and colors in the dark. It was spontaneous, where you just write everything you see, hear and feel both on the outside and on the inside.

It was like a faucet we could open at will. It leaked at nights, every night, and we were flooded with words and rhythms. Eventually we would fall asleep, perhaps, and when we woke up that noon we remembered only seeing a black figure by our bed.

It had eyes of pure white. Blank Pages.

We got dressed and followed Y outside.

She was a new land to be explored.

"What are you going to do?" We said.

"About what?"

"About life. Now that you're here, out of home and..." We sat beside her.

"I don't know yet. I might sign up for drama lessons." Said Y.

"A worthy cause." Said we.

The day was windy and we were hungry. Y's light curls rode on the wind in waves of gold, a shining child. Everything seemed grey that day, except for her.

There was no sign of last night's rain.

"Who's Lucas?"

"You gotta meet him! You'll get along great together."

"Is that the guy you're sleeping at?"

Y nodded. "He's also a writer."

"He probably sucks."

"I don't know, he never showed me anything he wrote. Like you."

The café was humid and we took a quick mental sketch of the people in the room. The light was yellow and old guys were sitting by the tables. Nobody looked at us, they were all strangers, and we wondered if we could find anything interesting there.

A girl rose to her feet and waved, and Y hurried towards her. We shook her hand.

She smiled, but with her pink lips alone. "Nice to meet you."

Her younger sister was Y's friend from school. They were all small town girls.

We all sat down. Y sat next to us, dressed in a white oversized shirt that covered her breasts. Pink's hair was brown, and her bangs covered her eyebrows. Her nose was round and her lips were thick.

She was looking straight at us.

"Where's Lucas?" Said Y.

"He said he couldn't make it." Said Pink. "Work, or something."

"Too bad." Said Y. "He's the only other writer I know."

We and Pink were drinking beer. Her hands were on the table, not far from ours. We could reach out and touch them. When we raised our eyes from there we found Pink's eyes, pale brown.

Y was underage, so she settled for orange juice.

That's okay too.

"So, you're a writer." Said Pink. "That's interesting. What does it mean?"

"It means no money and an immature death."

Good joke. Everyone laughed.

"Don't tell me you're putting all your faith in writing." Said Pink.

Writing was everything. Or everything was writing.

"That's what you're supposed to do." Said we.

We gave up sleep and food and just wrote for hours. We wrote our dreams in such detail that they became real, and they were vivid in our mind for hours after we started our day. Sometimes we didn't really know if the things in our head really happened, or maybe they're just pieces of dreams that were left there.

"Lucas is like that too." Said Y.

"What book are you writing?" Said Pink.

"I don't even know if it's a book. Maybe it's just... something."

"So why do you write it, then?"

"Well, the only way to learn how to write is by writing." We said. "And you have to write everything that comes to mind without thinking about it."

We could not yet tell her why.

"How can you write without thinking?" Said Y.

"You let someone else do the thinking." We said.

"Why don't you go study writing, then?" Said Pink. "Like, at the university."

"I never pay for what I can get for free." Said we.

Pink choked on her laughter. She took another sip of beer, and her sad, big eyes never left us.

We felt like biting something soft.

"Will you tell me more about writing?" Said Pink.

"When you write something that's meant to be read, it has to engulf the reader and take him elsewhere. It also has to be very true, in that it goes deep inside the mind and emotion. When it's meant to be acted and viewed on screen, you stay on the surface most of the time, and it's shallower." We said. "Isn't it?"

We drank a lot of beer in that café, in front of those big, sad eyes. Otherwise we wouldn't have been able to talk that much.

"What about your life?" Y looked at Pink.

"Nothing. I'm at home all the time. He's just busy with his music and friends."

"Who's he?" Said we.

"My boyfriend." She looked at us. You couldn't mistake that stare.

"Why is he not here?" Said Y.

"Busy." Pink shrugged.

"So everyone left you today." We said with a smile.

"Yeah, they really did. I'm really bored." She looked at the ceiling.

"You can't write good stuff when your life is boring."

"Oh." She looked back at us. "So I guess your life is interesting, then?"

Y laughed. She knew nothing.

This is why we came to this city.

Inspiration, you see.

"Just a little." We said.

"Show me sometime." Said Pink.

"I will."

"You'll really love Lucas." Said Y and looked at the street.

People didn't look back. They were walking inside the wind. The whole street was like a wind tunnel. Those were the best of days.

"Yeah, you can talk about writing forever." Said Pink.

"What if he sucks?"

"What if you suck?" She said.

Y laughed again and got up. "I'm going to the restroom."

"We should get going anyway." Said we.

"Sure, when I get back."

"So..." Said Pink. "What makes your life so interesting?"

"Take a walk with me and I'll tell you. It's not something that you can just explain in words."

"Okay. Sure." Said Pink. "Where to?"

"I know a really beautiful place." We said.

She chuckled.

When Y came back we all went out, and the sun was setting behind the buildings of this city.

"Nice meeting you." We told Pink.

"You too." She said and looked at Y. "And your parents keep asking my sister about you." Pink rolled her eyes.

"Oh, I'll come back. They worry too much." Said Y.

"They worry that you might do something... dangerous." Said Pink.

Too late.

We wanted raw meat.

And as we walked in the windy sunset, all the people were frozen. Y walked ahead between them, her shirt dancing like a white, blank page.

Someone had told her we were writing.

Someone had sent her to us.

And we were willing to accept.

Seems like she wanted to stay.

Now remember, she came to us.

And Death never sleeps.

You will understand it all, when the time comes.

Writing is a ritual, if you stick to it. It's the first thing you do in the morning, and it's the last thing you do at night. At home or outside, in the bookstore, when it's raining or when it's not. Nothing else matters. You take a sharp pen and you engrave wet ink on the pages, and you focus all your conscious and unconscious thoughts on it.

We entered the little cell in the early evening. Y jumped back. We peered over her shoulder, and saw the big cockroach above the bed.

And we killed it.

Every day we killed.

We threw the giant body in the trash can. There were a few others there. The place was infested.

Why would she stay here?

"Do you hear it?" Said Y.

We had one neighbor who was playing the piano. We've never met them, but the sounds were coming from behind the wall. By now you should know, our cell was small for a reason. It was a bigger apartment divided into two by the landlord. Barely legal, but satisfying.

Here we could draw ink and blood.

We looked at Y, who picked up a beer.

In the lobby of this building there was only one door, and behind it two doors. One was the main one, where the pianist neighbor lived. One was ours. The cell was simply carved inside the wall, and the triangular space between the two doors was so narrow you couldn't even have two people in there at the same time. You also couldn't close the outer door until you opened yours. We mean ours. Luckily, you weren't there.

The opening looked like a piece of the wall was just torn out by some wild beast.

In such a place, if you have a notebook, ink and blood, you can summon gods and demons to dance in the night. And we had all three.

Y can confirm this is all true, if you ever find her.

"That's really beautiful." She said of the music.

It really was.

She felt so comfortable there.

Too bad things ended up that way.

Outside, the wind still blew and the day was getting dark.

Y looked at us. We didn't even know why she was there. We let her in, yes, but why would she want to stay? She had other friends, like that Lucas guy, we knew that. She didn't spend every night in our bed.

Now she was drinking, and we joined her. We sat on the bed and made a line of empty bottles against the wall. Y looked at her hair in the mirror.

We saw ourselves behind her.

The mission was this: to take in all that is in this world and create something else. Make the temporary, eternal. It is the Magic of the word. And Magic never stays between the pages, if you do it properly.

What we really wanted to do was to stop time in its tracks, to preserve that which is passing, and to create a place for us to be free. Of course, this means recording everything. It also means dealing with Death, if you want to overcome it. It means others must also be touched by Death, whether they want to or not.

But Y came to us.

She wanted to.

And so we drank with her and kissed her, and when we couldn't resist the hunger any longer, we licked her like fire in her loins.

She was only fourteen at the time.

CHAPTER V

DO YOU KNOW WHAT A SHAMAN IS?

We were waiting for The Worm.

It was all muddy, endless water, with no bottom. Just this great puddle drowning the entire planet. No, this isn't something you will ever witness. It has already occurred. It was trillions of years ago. You weren't there. But we were. And we too were in this water, no up or down, just floating there. We were not alone. We are never alone. We were waiting for The Worm. It was a giant, naked, slithering thing. We haven't seen it, but we knew it was there, roaming, looking for prey. The Worm will digest you for a thousand years. We were waiting when we saw the flash of green. It was something big, not as long as The Worm, but still a giant. We saw its eye, and it was comforting. The Worm won't touch us now. Here comes its nemesis, our savior, the green Iguana.

We opened our eyes in bed that morning and wrote it down like mad. Lest we forget. We must record, and never forget. That is the mission, when these visions are sent to us.

We haven't seen Y for a whole week. That's just how things were between us. She came whenever she wanted, even though she still kept asking for permission every time, and we didn't ask any

41

questions. We had enough to write about, and we could already feel how we get deeper and deeper into that girl.

We shouldn't, mind you.

And one day our legs carried us to a big tree in the middle of the main street, not too far from the big mall, where we could read and write for hours. Under the tree was a little spice shop.

"You can go in. I'll be right there." Said the girl by the door, puffing out blue smoke from between her lips.

She was smoking and staring at the clouds. Everybody waited for the rain, but the rain didn't come so often. This is Middle Eastern winter for you.

"Oh. I didn't mean to go in."

She chuckled. "Then you should."

We peered inside. We didn't care much for spices. But the girl was barely dressed. Her hair was long and black and her skin was tanned, and it looked golden. Her right shoulder was covered with the face of an Indian chief, adorned with feathers. He looked at us as she came in.

"Are you from around here?" We said.

"No." Her narrow eyes pierced us. "And you're not, too."

"No one is."

She chuckled again.

That's how we met Puff.

"But you in particular look more lost than others." She said.

We walked in after her and our nostrils were flooded with every scent, from this world and others. That's what you might call "confusing the senses". It was a soup of all smells that filled the little room. The shelves almost reached the ceiling, and she was too short and too small.

"I use a ladder." Said Puff as we looked. Her ass was moving from side to side as she went behind her counter. "Wanna take a puff? It'll be good for ya."

"Do you just smoke it here? What if someone comes in?"

"I offer them a puff." Said Puff.

"What if they're cops?" We said and leaned on the counter.

She was rolling another one for later.

"Cops," Puff raised her eyes at us. "Smoke the whole joint."

We looked at her licking it. Her fingers were short and she had several different rings and a thin gold chain around her neck. Her black tank top had a deep cleavage but her breasts were very small, almost nonexistent. She had a golden ring in her navel.

But then she turned around to put the joints in her bag.

Her back was covered with a big tattoo of a winged woman, with her legs covered by the thin tank top. We wanted to see more.

"So what are you looking for?" Said Puff.

"Inspiration." We said. "I'm a writer."

"Oh! Came to look for inspiration in the big city?"

"Something like that." We said.

"Like all the great ones. You should pay attention."

And then she got out from behind the counter and went to help the old lady that came in behind us. The place was small and we could hear the cars outside. Tel Aviv is always doing something. If you pay attention, you can catch her right as she does.

The old lady went out without looking at us.

Puff did. Her eyes were small, dark, and piercing.

43

"You look tired."

"I don't sleep much." We said.

"Wanna tell me about it?"

"Just... dreams." We said. Other worlds. Other bodies.

"Oh." Said Puff and raised her eyebrows. She got behind the counter again.

"They're very vivid. Almost like now."

"Okay." Said Puff. "Do you know what a shaman is?"

"A spiritual leader of the Indians?" We said. The chief on her shoulder looked at us again. "A healer or something."

She chuckled and tapped on our hand.

"Let's go out for a smoke."

We followed her back to the entrance, and Puff started smoking again. "A shaman does all the things you said." She said. "But that's not what a shaman is."

"Go on."

This girl definitely knew something.

"A shaman is a link between this world and the spirit world. Understand? There are things you don't see with your eyes. They're out there." Puff wiggled her ringed fingers in front of us. "The shaman lets them possess him, so they can communicate with our world."

We bit our lip. "Do you believe that?"

"Yeah. It's true." She exhaled blue smoke. "But it takes a lot of spiritual work. It's ecstasy. They get ecstatic. They dance and jump and they take certain substances. Understand?" She said. "They go wild."

"It sounds like a seizure." We said.

"You see?" Said Puff. "That's exactly what people like you say. It's just a seizure. But it's not."

"Did you ever meet one?"

Puff put out her cigarette on the sidewalk and went in the shop, and we followed.

"Nope." She said. "Unfortunately."

"Maybe someday you will." We said.

"I don't think so." Said Puff. "Not in this city. I'm coming!" She looked over our shoulder and hurried to the old man who came in.

It is true. Some things are not seen by the eye. You know that. Then you write them down to give them a shape and form.

But we couldn't tell her we know that.

The old man lingered on and on, but she stayed beside him, smiling and whispering words. We never had that kind of patience. We had to run forward, to beat Death. To see everything. To be king.

We looked around the shop for a while but realized it's going to take her too long. We had our notebooks as always, and we had a lot to write about. As we got out we waved at her, and Puff said "sorry" with her lips behind her customer's back, and blew us a kiss.

We got out to the street and looked at all the people. Walking stories. No one looked at us. We looked up but there was not a cloud in the sky. A bird flew above us. It was an early evening and the sun was nowhere to be seen.

A shaman is one who transmits messages from other worlds. To do this, he has to lose his rational and orderly side and become a beast of prey. He has to use substances and dance.

Alcohol and nightclubs.

Pay attention.

Walk the path. N.

The graffiti on the wall was yellow lines.

When you write, it's just a symbol. Remember: a letter is nothing but a random drawing with an agreed upon meaning. You take one such symbol and group it with another, and you get a word. Several words and it's a sentence. Then another one and another one, and an abundance of sentences is a lifetime. But just like a table is made of atoms that are made of nothing, so does every text has meaning only in our heads, and without it, it is nothing.

Now you see the Magic in it. The Magic of Nothing, becoming Something. Chaos becoming Order. Meaning out of Nowhere.

So don't let anyone tell you that writing is simply putting words on paper. No, it is far ancient than that. Far stronger. And far more evil.

Walk the path. N.

The letters were drawn by someone. N.

He was the one signed on the first writing, too. The writing we saw at The Blue Bar the other night. The one we kept thinking about.

And as if the letters were goading us, our legs began walking. We walked and walked until we arrived at the wooden steps. The Blue Bar was real. Its door was open.

"There you are." Said Blondy as we went up. "We're just starting."

"What's going on today?"

"An open mic night. Every Sunday. You should come."

We sat by the bar while Blondy kept on wiping the glasses.

He put one of them in front of us.

We ordered a beer. The world was not enough.

"Have you been to the south of the city already?"

"What's there?"

"Clubs. Weird scenes." Blondy raised his eyebrows. "Don't stay in one place. Unless it's here, of course."

People filled the place and the first performer went on stage to start the evening. The shadows grew thicker on the walls, and we were starting to feel this body fade away. We got up and swayed around, listening to the music and looking at the stage. The place became very crowded, and we tried to find a path.

Then we hit a small table. A small empty glass fell on the floor. The pieces were stars beneath us, and we picked one up to examine it. Everyone looked at the stage, they were lost in music. We were never there.

But as our hand pulled the glass on our palm, a bright red surfaced as a proof of our body. We went back to the bar to get a napkin.

"Don't drink too much." Said Blondy.

But we couldn't help it.

Someone else was drinking.

And when we went to the restroom, the black inscription on the red ceiling was absolutely clear.

Walk the path. N.

We stood over the toilet and stared at the ceiling for we don't know how long. Our blood was golden whiskey and the world shrunk to this room only, to what our eyes can see and what our mind can contain. A myriad of images.

A myriad of writings on the walls. But this one was the most important one, and we didn't know why. Call it a gut feeling. There were phone numbers and names and all kinds of slogans, but only one writer there told us to walk the path.

And we knew the path.

Say "yes", and ye shall be redeemed.

Someone knocked on the door. "What's going on in there?"

We looked at our dick. It was just there, lax, dry of piss. We closed our fly and flushed the toilet, and opened the door.

It was a tall, slender man, wearing sunglasses and a black lipstick. We got out and got back in The Blue Bar. The stage was occupied by someone drumming a bass guitar and the loud thuds were making our blood bounce.

Blondy leaned towards us. "Where were you?"

"I was reading the writings in your restroom." We said without looking at him.

"Found anything interesting?"

We thought about it as we left and walked through the orange street, where the people came out to play all night, and the cars were stopping in front of the red traffic lights, and moving when they turned green.

We were surrounded by people. By the whole human safari. And we walked through it to our hole in the wall, looking at the streetlights and the signs along the way.

Walk the path.

There was our building. Our burrow. The night was staring without making a sound. We took the narrow walkway that led from the street to the building itself. The lights were casting long shadows, and their touch was stimulating. Death rose beside us, striding in long, silent steps towards the building door.

And as we entered the small lobby, Y was waiting there.

CHAPTER VI

❧

INVITED BY A BOOK

Yฺou should know by now, we are many.

And we will take control of this body.

As we sat on the bed that morning it took us a few moments to remember.

Last night the room was spinning, and the empty bottles were proof of it. Beer was liquid bread, so we didn't have to buy food.

We were trying to understand if drinking might give us some insight.

However, our notebook wasn't very readable that morning.

We went down to the bookstore at the mall. We had free time until the evening shift, which starts in the early afternoon. We intended to use it wisely. The bookstore was unique in that it also functioned as a library. We could sit there for the whole day to read and write, and it was better than writing in the cell.

There are several types of writing: in the morning it's recording dreams, and that should be done in bed. After a night out, it's better done inside as well, behind closed doors, in silence. The first thing that must be done when coming back to this world, is writing down all the details from the other worlds.

Some types of writing however, are better done in public places, where you can see and hear all that happens. It was Rimbaud, again, who talked about becoming a seer through the derangement of all the senses. It means you must say "yes" to everything and go wherever it leads you. You must travel and move and do a lot, and never stay in one place or your eyes and ears and fingers will get accustomed to it. Once you're accustomed to something, you can't see or hear anything.

We wrote notes for ourselves as we flipped the pages.

Thursday Night. C-U.G.2200. N.

That wasn't ours.

It was N's.

We stared at it, engraved in the inner margins of the book we took from the shelf.

It was a code. We were sure of it. But it was also meaningless.

Also, someone's damaging the books in the store, apparently.

Someone should be hanged for it.

Thursday Night. C-U.G.2200. N.

N...

"Sir?"

We looked at her.

"You know, you're not allowed to copy parts off of books." She said.

"I didn't. I'm just writing." We said.

"Okay, I'm just making sure."

She walked away.

The mall was huge and had entrances and exits to all four directions. We got out to the main street going southwest. At the end of it was The Blue Bar. But on the way there was the little spice shop.

Puff was coming out just as we were about to enter.

"Hey, love." She hugged and kissed us. Then her eyes pierced us. "Now what's on your mind?"

"Do you know what C-U.G. is?"

"Is this a trick question?"

We didn't know what to say.

Is this a trick question?

"Come inside, take a seat, and tell me everything." She said.

We sat there with her, by the counter, and prayed no one would interrupt us. She was wearing, as usual, a piece of cloth barely covering her orange skin. There wasn't much else to cover anyway.

"Something's bothering you."

"I don't sleep much." We said.

"Well, yeah. But what is it? What is C-U.G.?"

Maybe she knows something. Maybe she knows everything. And so, we decided to tell her of the weird writings. We've seen them four times by now. Twice at The Blue Bar, in the restroom. Once on a wall.

There was one right near the shop, we remembered, but we haven't even checked if it's still there.

Why wouldn't it be?

And we've seen it a fourth time, now, in a book.

"Why are they so special? It's just someone writing on the wall. Everybody does that in bar toilets." Puff chuckled.

"I don't know. It's just that I remember it more than the others." We said. "Other writings seemed normal, in a place like that."

"There's nothing normal in a place like that." Said Puff. "Is that what keeps you from sleeping? Writings on the wall?" She laughed.

We shrugged and looked at all the jars above our heads. The smell was intoxicating, mesmerizing. We could almost not find the exit, which was right in front of our eyes.

Writings on the wall.

She was right, wasn't she?

No.

There were other things keeping us from sleeping.

"You're very keen on finding out what C-U.G. is, aren't ya?" Said Puff. "You said Thursday night? If they gave a date it can be a place... so maybe it's a building."

"Well, you know anything?"

"Depends on who you're asking." She laughed. "Come on, remind me of that writing again."

"C-U.G.2200."

"2200 is the hour, baby. Thursday night, ten PM."

This time she was right.

Puff walked over to the entrance and looked at the sky. She puffed on her joint and let out blue smoke, invisible against the background of clear sky.

"So it's a day and an hour." We joined her.

"And a place."

Sounds like it.

Puff's eyes were searching the sky, the tree, and the pavement.

"Thursday night is the weekend. Sounds like a party."

Or maybe she just needed one.

"Where do you have parties?" She chuckled as she looked at us. "At clubs!"

"Where do you get all that?"

She showed us her joint. "Clear mind. Let's you see the truth."

"Where are the clubs, then?"

"The shady ones? The ones that people would write about in codes inside of books?" She looked at us with a crooked smile. "The southern part of town, of course."

"Hello, sweetie." An old woman approached, and we cleared the way for her to enter the shop.

Puff put out her joint and hurried inside after her. While this was happening, we checked on the graffiti near the shop. There was no N. there was nothing. As if it was never there.

We strolled back inside, thinking. Even if it wasn't meant for us, it'll probably be a good idea to go there. We mean a bad idea. But bad ideas can inspire you just as well as the good ones.

Going out at night was kind of both.

The old hag never left, though. She asked more and more questions and filled her nylon bags with all kinds of ingredients. Spices, nuts, everything that Puff had to offer.

Almost everything.

Strange, how we can't seem to remember what the old hag was wearing, or what she looked like. She's probably long gone by now. Hunched over those jars, inhaling all the scents...

She looked at us then, and her eyes were pure white. Blank pages.

"Oh." She said in recognition.

Maybe she was a guest at the hotel.

"Oh." Her finger waved towards us.

We and Puff looked at each other.

"You're a writer, aren't you?" Said the old hag.

"Of course he is!" Said Puff. "He has an amazing book coming out soon."

"Oh." Said the old hag as she examined our face. "Oh! You don't know who you are yet. Oh, no, you don't."

"He really doesn't." Said Puff.

A real savior.

"Oh, you don't." Said the old hag, looked at puff and picked up her bags. "Thank you so much, sweetie."

Puff laughed when she left the store. "See? Possession."

"She's possessed by something, that's for sure."

"You'd better believe it, baby."

We do.

And you should, too.

We left the shop that day and told Puff we'll keep her updated.

"Promise?" Said Puff. "And will you come visit me again? I'm bored here, all alone."

"Sure."

This wasn't over yet. But first we went straight to the bookstore. We had to make sure, and the clerk hurried towards us as we entered.

"Oh." She said. "Are you looking for anything specific?"

"Just the book I was reading."

"Please don't copy anything. Really." She said.

We took the book out of the shelf and sat down again. It was... magnetic, almost.

We searched through the pages.

Thursday night. C-U.G.2200. N.

We couldn't find the inscription.

We went over the entire book, but it just wasn't there.

"Ouch."

A paper cut.

Our blood was bright red.

As we raised our eyes the clerk was peeking from behind her counter, her eyes begging us to not stain the pages.

Even though, you know, blood should stain pages.

It's better than ink.

It also tastes better.

Believe us.

As we left for the hotel we remembered Blondy talked about clubs at the southern part of the city. And so one night, not too far away from Thursday, we asked him about it.

"Like, what kind of clubs?" Blondy looked at us.

"The... shady ones."

"There's a strip club right out on the street..."

"That's not what I meant." We said. "Just a place to dance."

"Oh, there are several."

And Blondy named them.

Club Under.Ground.

"Is that an actual place?" We stopped him.

It took us a second to figure out why.

Club Under.Ground.

"Yeah, it's an actual place. But it has a lot of regulars, so you shouldn't go alone. And you should behave according to their rules." Blondy gestured at his own bar. "Just like we're doing in here."

C-U.G.

Club Under.Ground.

22:00.

It was there. On Thursday night, but it was there.

We don't know why we were so certain, but we were.

The only thing left unclear was, who is N.

Well, we had to say "yes". You know we had to.

And we thought of Y.

She left home to find an adventure, didn't she?

Seems like we have found something that might be good enough.

And anyway, the ritual works best if she too is confused, deranged.

We'll take her along.

We knew they'd be waiting for us.

CHAPTER VII

~

UNDER.GROUND BEASTS

It was Thursday night.

Walk the path.

"What's inside?" said Y.

"No idea. Let's find out."

We stood on the street and the night was clear, and we could walk among the stars. We only hoped they'd let her in and won't ask about her age.

We wanted to blend in the dark and be a lizard on the wall, and watch her, and wait.

We got in line with her and as if nobody noticed, we found ourselves descending into the dark rooms, into the warm body of people. At first we only saw the lights and the music, and we let ourselves wander.

When we saw the bar, we made our way to it. Y looked around as if she couldn't tell dream from reality. She looked at all the people, and then looked at us.

For some reason, we smiled.

We've seen it all in the alleys of south Tel Aviv inside this nightclub full of darkness, with goat shadows prancing on the walls. Someone was whipped on stage. People were dancing around it. On the sofas, people were crawling on all fours or being stepped on. The music was swirling in this carnival of human safari. And we were there to look at it.

All the animals come out at night. People clad in black and corsets, white contact lenses, holding whips or glasses of beer. A long haired blond stared at us with eyes that seemed flat, acne scars deforming his face. When we looked again he was gone. We felt as if in a dream.

Maybe we finally fell asleep in our bed. Maybe the inability to sleep and the scratching of the roaches was about to kill us.

But Y was there, too.

"Who are these people?" She said.

We lowered our eyes at her from our place on the stool. Is she a dream too? If not, she will be. Through her we can reach eternity.

"Seems like we found something." We said.

The people were forming a circle.

The main show has begun.

Y tried to see what they're gathering around but she was too short.

"I'm gonna take a closer look." She said and walked between the black figures. Swaying, wobbly, otherworldly reflections.

Now more than ever she looked so lost we almost regretted bringing her there. She, just like us, was very far away from home.

We didn't know anyone there. They had no faces. They were all white and dressed in black, tall and thin and dancing. They were waiting for their shaman to begin. Y was easy to notice: her golden curls were a sun in the darkness. She didn't push her way forward, she was very patient and her legs walked as if they didn't want to reach there. They didn't want anything to do with that.

We understood.

After all, you remember, we didn't want any part of that too. But we gave permission to other forces to lead us to our goal. Sometimes you have to stare into the abyss if you wish to cross it. It always looks back.

Always.

Every time.

And so, the only thing to do was get some whiskey in our veins.

"Use a coaster." Said the bartender and put one in front of us.

Our hand froze in the air above it, just as we were about to put the glass down. Instead, we just looked at the writing on the round cardboard.

We will kill you. N.

The words were etched on the cardboard. Handwritten. The letters wiggled like worms.

We decided to go to Y. We broke through the circle and saw her golden hair.

On stage was a woman chained to a St. Andrew's Cross, and a big man was scratching her back with long, dirty nails. We couldn't see her face, but we saw the whip as he flung it. And we heard the cry of pain and pleasure.

Her white flesh was spotted with red, her wrists chained, and her fingers grabbed the cross every time he hit. She was no more than an animal, and the crowd was full of beasts. We watched as he flicked his cigarette on her ass, leaving stripes of ash, sending orange sparks into the air.

The human safari is full of beasts.

And it was feeding time.

We hugged Y from behind to let her know we were there, in one form or another. And our tongue wanted to shoot out into her, to eat her alive. Our arms squeezed her.

We looked to our left and saw guys in tight leather pants, their cocks stiff beneath the clothes. We saw the same to our right. Everyone wanted to fuck someone.

Then break them and leave the pieces there, so that they can assemble themselves into a new shape. Y looked at us and she wasn't smiling, but her face was confused and her eyes pierced straight into us.

"I'm going to the restroom."

"Are you okay?" Said we.

"Yes."

She never admitted her unease. She wanted to be an adult. Y thought she was more mature than her age group.

Well, she wasn't.

We looked at the markings on the girl's back. They can form words, which can form other worlds.

We got back to our seat and ordered another whiskey. Bringing Y was a mistake. A part of us felt sorry for her. We decided to drown it in liquid fire.

We will kill you. N.

When we raised our eyes from the coaster, two pure white eyes stared right back. Blank pages. The pale boy straightened his red bowtie, and lifted his top hat. "You're the new guy." He said.

He knew we were coming.

"Are you here alone?" Said Boy.

"I'm never alone." We said.

We are never alone.

"I love this place. These people are home."

He and the bartender smiled at each other, as if they were saying something without saying it. Something like, "He's the guy."

"What are you doing here?" Said Boy.

"I'm a writer. I'm searching for..."

"Inspiration." He said. "Just like me."

"Are you a writer?"

"We all are."

We looked at the people surrounding us. They all knew we were strangers. They crowded together like a human wall. They were mean eyes and leather.

It was feeding time.

We ordered our third glass of whiskey. We looked at the coaster.

We will kill you. N.

"You know, you can find anything in this city. If you walk the path." Said Boy. "I wander through the streets at night. You should too. You'll find a lot to put on paper there."

Coming to the city wasn't all about Inspiration. It was about getting away and creating a new life. And it wasn't only about writing a book, but of bending space and time.

"Writing is a ritual, you know. And in every ritual you have to sacrifice something. Time, other things." Said Boy. "Don't you think it's magic?"

"It is if you make it so."

"Think of the old days." Said Boy. "Back then they knew they can change reality with words. They wrote them down to make the changes permanent."

This boy knew too much. It was horrible.

Unfortunately, now you know too much as well.

"They wrote the words on paper. They called them talismans." Said Boy.

Our fourth glass of whiskey was yellow as piss.

We will kill you. N.

"They're incantations." Said we.

"They can hurt, or even kill you." Said Boy.

"They can kill you too." We looked at him.

Boy didn't flinch. "But you know what's really gonna help you?" He took out a bag of powder from his inner pocket.

He mixed it in a glass of water. No one seemed to notice, or care. The people weren't moving, just his hands as he stirred the water. They got a yellow shade, like piss.

"What is it?" We said.

"Poison." Said Boy.

Y stepped out from the human wall and put her hand on our arm.

"Oh." Boy looked at her. "Do I know you?"

Her eyes begged us to leave, but her mouth said, "No. Nice to meet you."

"I'm pretty sure I've seen you somewhere."

He looked around as if searching for something. Or someone. He gulped and his eyes came back to us. "Will you stay?"

We will kill you. N.

One look at Y was enough. Also, N's message was pretty clear this time.

No more riddles.

"No. We're leaving." We showed him our glass and took a long sip.

As we did this, we slid the coaster in our pocket. We got up from our seat and the human wall moved a little, like tree leaves in the breeze, but not more than that. They were towering above us, just staring.

"Are you here every Thursday?" We said.

"Maybe. And if not, my family is."

"Family." We looked at them.

Their eyes were pure white. Blank pages.

Boy drank his yellow piss in one sip, and the lights went out. For a moment we just saw the eyes. Then everything was submerged in darkness. The music was long gone, and we took Y by the hand and crawled through tunnels full of closed doors. We breathed the dark. It was cool as swampy waters, comforting. We were a lizard that night, and as we got out to the cold of way past midnight it was raining, and we stood beneath a tin roof listening, trying not to fade away. The tin was moaning over us. It hosts gods and demons.

How much did we drink? And what?

Well, we drank everything we could find.

We were living on beer, baked beans and ink.

"That was fun, wasn't it?" We looked at Y. "What did you think?"

"I think we should go home."

Funny. The hole in the wall became a home. It was just a place to rest for us, to hide when we needed it. To perform our rituals.

Boy talked about Magic.

He knew too much.

But he wasn't N.

"How did you find out about this party?" Said Y.

We were invited to this party by a book.

"Some guy at work." We said.

We thought of Puff. That was close enough. She really was at work when we asked her.

Now the water drenched all the dirt, and the garbage cans and bags started leaking between the cracks. Painting them black. The road was now a raging river through the city. Cars were throwing water at us but we were safe and untouched. The light also failed to reach us.

"Let's take a walk." We said.

"A long one?"

"As long as possible."

Tel Aviv keeps on going and we follow. It doesn't even matter where. You just say "yes" and follow. And all the people there were strangers looking for the edge of night under rickety tin roofs, through the city lights.

We stopped when all was dark. The rain became a slight dripping from roofs and drainpipes. Starless, glowing skies reflected through the puddles. Light could not reach this alley. A single lamplight was shining in the distance, beyond the haze. An eye of orange. A sun in the dark. The rain on the road split like white cobwebs.

But it was only sewage, after all.

We looked at Tel Aviv.

Tel Aviv stared right back.

And as we passed by the thin, ragged man in the alley, his sign read "We will kill you. N."

Our way home was longer than it should have been, and it was shrouded in a haze. We were in a world of smoke that the streetlights turned orange. A different planet.

We were used to it, though.

We never let go of Y's hand. We still needed her. But also, we just wanted to feel her warmth. In that rainy night, it was an anchor. Something to keep us from losing our body. We drank so much we were almost gone.

"Look." Y pointed.

An ad on a power box said, "The Meaning of Life Is Reality Check."

Reality check. That's what you do when you think you might be dreaming, like right now. We counted our fingers just to make sure. Dreams came to us vividly and we could see them in front of us as we lay awake in bed and cemented them in our notebooks. It was weird, seeing this reminder on the street. Who is it for?

It wasn't signed "N."

Maybe it wasn't meant for us, after all. N. We saw it too many times. Except for the party, none of it made any sense. But still, someone, some N, left us messages in public places. We stood there for a moment, still looking at the ad.

Y smiled at us. Looks like the air made her feel better. She squeezed our hand.

Boy didn't try to kill us. Lucky man. But he was of our kind. Why would he be "N"? Maybe it was someone in that club. Boy said they are all writers. Our kind.

Still, we were sure we can figure out the messages. After all, this whole thing has to make sense eventually.

Pay attention.

In front of us towered the mall, all full of lights and the letters in the electronic signs kept changing, red letters on black.

Now on sale! 2+1!

Inside, people were in the theater watching movies, unaware of anything happening outside.

New Products! We await you!

"Do you like it?" Said Y.

Find us, or we will find you! ;)

We could barely hear her. We looked down at the little girl.

"I'm just watching." We said.

We will kill you. N.

"I'm sorry I didn't want to stay."

"It's okay."

We saw enough.

Now, when it is written, a new world arises.

"Let's go do something else." Said Y.

"Whatever you want." We said with a smile.

CHAPTER VIII

~

LONG HAIRED BLOND

We looked at her neck, and we were hungry.

A thin golden chain was wrapped around it.

"I draw. Sometimes." She said. Pink lips.

Her neck led to her breasts, hidden behind a buttoned shirt.

"What do you draw?" Said we.

"Just... what I see." Said Pink.

We raised our eyes to hers.

"But if you're home all day, what do you see?"

She chuckled.

But her eyes remained sad.

We had to keep our hands in our pockets.

Pink came from a small town too, we reminded ourselves. Now she was living with her boyfriend in Tel Aviv and was looking for a job. Everyone was couples except for Y and us.

"I don't know what I want to do." She said. "I just want to draw."

She seemed lost enough.

"What about your boyfriend?"

Pink shrugged. We could see she was looking everywhere but us, and she probably drank too much. We had an urge to drink more than her, and she had an urge to do the same, and so we were both drinking for the past two hours.

But we handled it better.

After all, we are many.

"We don't get to hang out much." Said Pink. "My drawing teacher arranged an exhibition for me last month, and he didn't even come. He was busy with something."

"Well, now you're here." We said. "I'll show you a place I like."

"Let's go." She said.

We paid and got out to the street. It was an early afternoon, and we started walking in the direction of the hotel. We didn't really want to go there after the morning shift, but we wanted to get Pink.

And so we were walking south and she was walking where we walked. We crossed the main boulevard and went into the smaller streets. Here there were fewer cars, fewer people. We could fuck or kill anyone.

"Y spends a lot of time at your place."

It sounded true enough.

"She needs a place to sleep. She sleeps at your place, too, isn't she?"

"Yeah, sometimes. Or at Lucas's. We're not far away from each other."

"I still haven't met this guy."

"You really should. He writes all the time."

That meant something. When you write all the time, you have no choice but to gain some knowledge of the craft. Of its antiquity, of its power...

"He says that's his ritual." Pink looked at us.

"What about your boyfriend? Why don't you leave?" Said we.

People are thrown into this world like tamed animals, and they do whatever they're told whenever it's possible, drifting like the leaves on the boulevard we left behind. They stick to what they know best, cling to the people they find around them even if they were originally uninvited.

Have you ever found yourself in a certain place with certain people, and wondered how did you get there?

"He's working, it's important." She said, but her eyes were desperate.

They were all friends in the big city. We were the outsiders.

Luckily for her, she wasn't locked in our cell with us.

Trust us. This is nothing like what you may think. Y was fourteen, and we knew we have no future with her. There couldn't be. She was lost, but she didn't show it much. Or we didn't dare looking. Y was trying very hard to be strong and mature, and that was reasonable. All her friends were older.

We are ancient.

"We need to get there before sunset." We said.

Hand in hand we walked through the small streets as Pink told us of her life alone at his house.

"Wow." She said when the towering hotel was revealed, watching the park and the sea. That's where we went.

We crossed the road and the park, left the hotel behind us, and sat on the rocks above the water. When the waves crashed they sprinkled us with warm, salty drops. The sun was orange and almost touching the Mediterranean.

"How do you know this place?" Said Pink.

We pointed. "I work at the hotel."

"Oh. I thought you were a writer."

"I thought you were a painter." We retorted.

Pink laughed. She leaned on us, and we kissed her and felt her tongue and teeth. The sun was shining on the water, and we went north towards the beach. The sky grew darker, and some yellow plastic chairs were scattered on the sand.

We didn't sit.

Instead, we grabbed Pink and pinned her to a brick wall, and her tongue was in our mouth. We don't even remember what she wore, but all we wanted was to take it off.

She didn't let us.

We grabbed her breasts, her thighs, her neck... it was fragile. We pressed a little, we don't know why. She was in our hands, but we were not done with her yet. And even though she tried to protest, Pink was still kissing us.

At first there was no one else there but the stars. And the stars were pairs of eyes, but they couldn't tell anyone any secrets. And they've seen many secrets in the nights of Tel Aviv.

We could have taken her there. If not there, somewhere else. Another time. If we were out of the cage, believe us, we would have been a lot more difficult to handle.

But she didn't want to go on.

She saw him staring.

"Lucas?" Said Pink.

"Oh, hey, it's you." He said. "I... I wasn't sure. Hi."

He approached us. Pink and we separated and she gave him a friendly hug. As he shook our hand we recognized him. A long haired blond with acne scars. We felt as if in a dream.

Lucas was at the club on Thursday night.

"So you're Lucas." We said.

"Hi... Nice to meet you." Said Lucas.

Apparently Y was talking. He knew we were writers and he knew she sleeps at our place from time to time. We didn't know what else she told him.

"I need to be home soon." Said Pink. "Will you two walk me there?" She looked at us.

"Lead the way." We said.

"It's the same place... right?" Said Lucas. "I... I know the way."

We left the beach behind us and went east, back into the streets and alleys on our way to south Tel Aviv.

"Um, so how do you two know each other?" Said Lucas.

"From the time you bailed out on us, a week ago." Said Pink.

"It was two weeks ago." Said we.

"Oh, yeah. I... I had to finish something at work. Um." He said.

"What work?" We said.

"It's hi-tech stuff." Lucas waved his hand as if it's unimportant. "Too bad I couldn't make it."

He was slouching as he walked. Lucas wore plain clothes, a blue shirt and cargo pants full of pockets. They seemed full.

The night settled in the alleys and the buildings were tall. Tree leaves were frozen on their branches. The lamplights flooded the street with orange lights, creating long shadows in the street corners.

"Tell me about your writing." Said Pink.

Lucas and we looked at each other, then at her.

We could kill her to leave no witness.

"I think..." He said. "I think... when you write on paper, um, with a pen, you... you change stuff."

Pay attention.

"Um, it's like an incantation. Or a talisman. When you write it. All you have to do is collect the right words at the right time. And if you take every feeling and thought of the mind and transcribe it in every moment in time, there's nothing separating this written consciousness from that of the flesh. It's like an analog preservation of yourself."

In other words, pun intended, we can write a mind to eternity, completely.

Or so goes the theory.

We found ourselves nodding. Someone gets it, and he's Y's friend.

He's Lucas.

"Oh." Said Pink.

"Um... Sorry. I was rambling." Said Lucas.

He was now ahead of us and we only saw his hunched back and the orange lights. We were walking on the road. There were houses to our left and bushes to our right, and the street had a minor incline.

"You... you should move out of this neighborhood." He said.

"What's wrong with it?"

Pink rolled her eyes at us, behind his back.

"Um... there are... you know, uh, predators walking around."

She mouthed his words as he said them.

"You're the only one walking around." Said Pink. "Both of you."

"Hm."

Lucas just kept on walking. He was a writer, after all.

He had other worlds to worry about.

Pink was walking next to us. Her shadow was moving on the road to our right, and when we looked at her she looked away.

She shrugged. "It's okay. And I'm not afraid of getting raped." Pink looked at his back.

"You shouldn't be." We said.

"Yeah, maybe I want it, even." She said.

"Well, if you want it, it's not rape." We looked at her.

"If I wanted it," Pink smiled at us. "Would you have raped me?"

Believe us, we are not to be teased or tested. It brings us closer to freedom.

Lucas turned around and pointed at the building.

"It's... it's here, right?" He said.

"Yeah." Said Pink. "You remember."

"See?" Smiled Lucas, like a kid who got praise.

Pink hugged us and we could feel her breasts. The body that got away. She disappeared in the dark stairwell and she was gone. Now we were left alone with Lucas, the guy who knows about fetish clubs and writing.

He was staring at us with flat eyes.

"I live not far away." Said Lucas.

"I'll walk with you." Said we.

"So how do you know Y?" He said as we walked.

"Through a friend." We said. "You?"

"The same." Said Lucas. "Sometimes we go out to eat."

"Us too." We said. "There's a great burger place not far from my place."

"Oh, I don't eat that." Said Lucas as he curled a strand of light hair around his finger. "I'm... I'm a vegan for several years. So... so I don't. Um."

"It's okay. Your loss."

"I still have great food." Said Lucas. "And besides, drinking is better. I usually go out every night."

"What about work?"

"You can't let work destroy your day." Lucas chuckled. "I'm always looking for fun stuff to do."

"Me too." We said.

"To be honest, I'm kind of a hedonist, myself." said Lucas. "Um."

"How can you be a hedonist?"

"What do you mean?" He said. "Pleasure is at the top of my priorities."

"But you don't eat meat." We said.

Lucas stopped and stared at us. "But I can enjoy other things..."

"Hedonism doesn't mean having fun." We said. "It means you only have fun, and you never give up pleasure. And you gave up certain kinds of food, right?"

"Hm..." he curled a strand of hair around his finger again. It was as if he was considering it. "Yeah. You're right."

We continued our walk for a while. We didn't know where he actually lives, and whether or not he's just dragging us through the streets. Lucas seemed disturbed, as if something was really bothering him. He didn't say a word until the street split into two, then he just stopped.

Write like you mean it. N.

It was smeared on a dusty wall.

"You see, that's what I'm talking about. Um." Said Lucas. "I mean... Um. You know."

"That's what you're supposed to do." Said we.

"Well, thanks for the... the walk." Said Lucas. "Good night. Oh, and... we'll see you again."

We nodded and watched him walk away for a minute or two.

All we could do was write. And as we wrote we saw and heard the words, and we were in a different world where everything we wish for, happens. Lucas was right about that and we knew it. The more we wrote the more the world changed, even in subtle ways. This was the only way, and the faster we'll make it, the easier it will be. But before it was easy, it had to be tough.

As he disappeared in the orange lights, a ghost, Death smiled.

Write like you mean it.

CHAPTER IX

❧

THE WRITING ON THE WALL

Write like you mean it. N.

We looked at the slim, wrinkled man chasing the pigeons.

Gideon was the dining hall manager, which means he didn't do much but check on us once in a while. He wasn't as loud as Fat Man, or as demanding as Little Boy, and he was slim and wrinkled. His hair was grey and his face was long as his fingers, and he was trying to get the pigeons out of his dining hall before anyone comes in.

The sun was getting lower. Its fingers grew longer and stretched towards us, near the dishwashing machine that's in the back, hidden from the hotel guests' eyes. The tables were all ready for dinner. The sea looked almost white beneath the yellow orb approaching it, and the dining hall was bathing in gold.

Gideon already managed to get one pigeon out, and now there was only one left. It was the daily ritual. The pigeon stood on the table next to one of the plates, and looked around with red eyes.

"He doesn't give up." Said tall Sally with her arms crossed.

She came from a small town too.

All the small town people gathered in this city. Became its living organism.

Waiter A and Waiter B came in to try and help Gideon. Waiter A was the guy we saw carrying the tray on our first day.

He was complaining to us one time, about the boss telling him to remove his nail polish before coming to work. "They don't understand me at all." He told us.

Now he was opening the window while old Gideon and Waiter B tried to chase the pigeon through it.

"Don't let the other one come back!" Said Waiter B.

Waiter A waved his hands at the pigeon that was trying to get back in.

"Aren't you supposed to help?" Said Sally and gathered her black-as-coal hair.

"No." Said we.

This is how things were at the hotel. The guests were loud and simple, eating away at their omelets and salads and cheese. Afterwards they would go to their rooms or wander the streets, but only where they can spend their time and money and live their uneventful lives. We wanted none of this.

It's been almost six months since we arrived in Tel Aviv. We learned the streets and alleys with our feet. They walked on their own. Sometimes we listened to the rain from within our cell. Sometimes Y was there, sometimes other things.

Death was present whenever we looked. And he was more prominent in the little cell, in the mirror, on the bed, crawling on the wall in the body of a cockroach. He was there as we cut our legs and the back of our palms, drawing blood.

Bright red.

We got dressed and went straight to the bookstore. We had to check.

The clerk nodded at us with pursed lips.

But we went straight for that book... the one that invited us to the Under.Ground.

And the book was pure white. Blank pages.

We only wanted to look for N's message, and the whole book was empty. No words, no sentences, no paragraphs.

"Are you okay?"

It wasn't the clerk.

It was the green eyed girl that stood there.

"You look a bit pale."

We don't get much sunlight, we suppose.

She climbed on her tiptoes to peek at the book. We waited. She looked at us.

"I'm sorry. You just... I thought maybe something was wrong."

Well, what do you call an empty book sitting on the shelf of a bookstore, lady?

She was short and thin, wearing a plain black shirt and holding her hands on her belly. She had a dark brown hair that barely reached her exposed shoulders, and she had thick eyebrows and green, round eyes.

She was staring.

She was still staring when we turned away and got back to our table. We took out a notebook and started working. The clerk looked too, just to make sure we don't have another book with us.

All those salespeople only interrupt with reading.

The new girl sat next to us with a book, but she didn't read it.

She was staring.

"You're a writer?" She said. "I know some writers."

Aren't we all?

"Are they good?"

"I don't know. I don't understand anything about it." She said.

"Lucky girl."

Not so much.

And that's how we met Alice, and everything started falling apart. Believe us, we never wanted any of this. We wanted to live and write, and to live a life worth writing. But we had to seek our Inspiration, bleed for it, die for it. Kill for it.

When you write, Magic happens.

She was a new land to be explored.

And everything new was worth trying at least once.

"What are you writing about?" She said.

"I... don't know yet." We said. "It's an experiment."

"With what?"

She was stubborn, but it was good. We reminded ourselves, and we remind you now, we have to say "yes" to this city.

"With life." We said.

The sky was getting dark outside and the lights in the street were beginning to shine.

And we found something to play with that night.

"Oh, here's Lucas." She waved.

We raised our head and we saw him. Standing there, twirling a strand of hair around his finger. The face of a little mouse.

"Um. Hi." He kind of waved.

He approached the table from its other side.

"I was just talking about you." Said Alice.

"Oh. Okay."

"Sit."

"No, no. I'm... in a hurry."

Tough crowd.

"I actually thought we could talk." Said we.

"Sorry." Said Lucas. "Um."

"What are you doing here?" We said.

"How do you guys know each other?" Said Alice.

We both looked at Alice, then at each other. Lucas was standing there, chewing his lip. We were sitting, pen frozen in our hand.

Write like you mean it. N.

"Through Y." He said. "You know... my friend."

"Oh!" Said Alice. "She's cute."

"Well, everybody knows everybody here." We said. "Or so it seems."

We don't say anything about love. You shouldn't think that. We only see opportunities and we say "yes" to them. That's all that matters.

Pay attention, this is not a love story.

Not even close.

"Wait a second." We told him.

"I really have to go..."

But we went over to the shelves and took the book out. The blank one. The clerk looked up to search for violations of any store rules.

We opened the book in front of him.

Blank pages.

Nothing.

"It's... blank." He said.

Then he raised his eyes to ours, as pale as a ghost, and took a step back.

"Show me!" Alice got up and leaned over the book. "Oh, it's a love poem!"

"Can you read it?" We said.

"Excuse me." The clerk was there, hands crossed on her chest. "Please be quieter, and don't damage the books."

"This book seems damaged." We handed it over to her.

Her eyes passed over the blank pages as if she was reading the words.

"There's no problem with the book." She said. "Now, are you reading it or not? Because if not, you should put it back on the shelf."

"It's unreadable." We said.

"Sir, this is a very famous and respected poet."

She really didn't understand. We sighed.

"Well, are you reading it? All of you?"

"No. You can keep it."

"Oh, no." She closed the book. "It's on sale!"

We looked at her going back to the shelves and putting it there. Then we looked at Lucas, and he was gone. He really was in a hurry.

He really was seeing weird things.

We had several things in common.

Never a good thing.

N said "write like you mean it", which means you actually see and hear the reality you're making. You put your soul in it.

But you didn't, luckily. It was us who did.

When we got out of the mall Alice was still there, talking about her psychology studies and college life. For us, the streets were life. We got on the main boulevard and walked side by side between the trees, which were staring like alien creatures. Their shadows swayed on the road and on her face.

It was dark.

Soon there will be monsters outside.

Well, there are, even now.

Alice will move away soon but she still didn't know where to. In the meantime she shared an apartment with a friend. We knew we can't go there, and so we needed to create a space just for us in the streets. The more we walked the fewer were the people. It was us who wished it to be so.

We led Alice to the side streets and found a bench to sit on. It was painted with orange light and no one could see us there.

We tried not to think of Lucas.

"Writing sounds interesting." Said Alice. She held her hands between her thighs.

"Only if you make it so." We said.

Alice chuckled. "Tell me a story."

"There was a writer named William S. Burroughs, and one time he and his woman were playing William Tell." We said the first thing that came to mind.

We could see it, the bar in the fifties. The desert landscape. Hot outside. The flies came in and out, and the bums were filling the bar.

"William Tell was the guy who shot an arrow through an apple that was on his son's head." We said. "So they did the same with a chaser glass and a gun. She put the glass on her head and he shot it."

"Wow." Said Alice. "Did he hit?"

"No. He missed the glass." We said. "But he hit his woman right between the eyes."

She swallowed hard.

The body dropped to the floor from the bar stool.

"He wrote a lot of good books. And he used a lot of cut-ups." We said. "That's when you take a finished text and cut it into pieces and put them back together. So they form a new story that's sort of an automatic story, which no one actually meant to write. And Burroughs said, when you cut into the present the future leaks out."

"What does that mean?" Said Alice.

We still can't tell you that, little girl.

But if you prove worthy, you will know.

The ritual is near.

Alice laughed, and we leaned forward and kissed her. She was surprised at first but her lips opened and our tongue was moving in her mouth. We pushed it as deep as we could get.

Then her green eyes looked at us and she was breathing heavily. But her hand was on our neck and she kissed us. There was no one else in the world.

We made sure of it, for the night.

We got up and started looking for a spot away from the street. We could do it right there, but she was embarrassed. Alice was rather shy but she had no choice other than to do as we wanted. And so we found a spot and started touching each other. We did most of it, and Alice was letting us do as we pleased.

"Don't you dare do anything!" Came a scream.

We stopped and looked, but there was no one there.

"Kids! I can see you behind that pillar! Don't do anything here!" The woman's voice screamed again.

Well, that's what windows are for, we guess. We didn't see her, but we laughed about it and went away. Alice was holding our hand and her warmth made us tingle.

She could be a great sacrifice for him.

"What's her problem?" She said.

She wasn't the type who'll push us behind a big, parking car and ride our cock near a basketball court.

"Do you want to do this another time?" Said Alice.

"No." We said.

Instead, we found a parking lot and sat with our backs to the stone wall. It was almost empty and enclosed between two buildings. They were far enough. Darkness filled the corners. We could kiss Alice and touch her as much as we wanted. And she let us.

Girls are easy if you want to.

Alice let us touch her breasts and kiss her neck and ear. Her hair was pricking our cheek and nose. Our hand rushed between her legs and started rubbing her pants, and she panted.

"No. No." She said. "Not here. Please."

We stopped only when she caught our hand, and went back to kissing her. But we took her hand and put it on our groin, and she stopped breathing.

"Come on." We said and pulled her hand inside our pants.

You have to do what you have to do. And you have to say "yes". And you have to write it all.

Her fingers closed around our cock and started rubbing it as we whispered in her ear. We whispered all about the other worlds, the visions... we had no idea if she can hear it. But we knew we can take her there, she just needed a little push.

And Death smiled.

We didn't let go. She was in our hands now and she knew it, like a deer in the headlights.

Her hand was moving up and down inside our pants and our cock was stiff. We put our hand on our groin, holding her hand in there. Hot cum flowed in our pants and wet our hairs and her fingers. We were looking at the stars, and they were pairs of eyes.

Alice looked at us like a scared animal. We wonder what she would have written about it, now that she had her own new, unique experience. This was obviously not her usual style, and she just went along with it. She said "yes". Just as she should have done.

"Oh God." She said.

We got back to the road still holding hands, but we stopped as we saw the writing on the wall. It was black graffiti, oozing.

Eternal life is N.igh

"What are you staring at?" She said.

"It's nothing." Said we. "Just... a strange feeling."

"Are you okay?"

"As usual." We told her.

The writings were our newest secret.

Well, ours and Lucas's.

CHAPTER X

Y

We'll be honest with you, we have no idea why she kept coming back.

But some days when we got off work, or sat at the mall reading, or just transcribed our visions in bed, Y would send us a message to ask if she could sleep in our cell. We knew she was too young, and yet we kept saying "yes", and kept telling her to come without asking. People come in all shapes and sizes, and in all ages.

We were surrounded by women, but somehow none of them stayed.

It was all in our head as we looked at Y, sitting on our bed that afternoon and messing with her cellphone. She came straight after school and the place became a little nicer to be in.

"Ugh!" She said.

We quickly squashed the cockroach that ran near her feet, and then took the body in a piece of toilet paper and threw it in the toilet.

"Why don't you do something with them?"

"There's nothing I can do." We said.

Maybe we were not in control as we thought we were.

N.

"Are you going to sleep here tonight?"

"I don't know yet." She smiled.

Y was wearing a white shirt and red pants. We wore nothing, as it wasn't necessary. At first Y wanted us to get dressed, but she got used to it. We sat beside her and started kissing her.

"Wait." She chuckled before we pushed her on her back.

"Who are you talking to?"

"It's Lucas." Said Y.

"So tell him you're busy." We said.

Y looked in our eyes. "Pink told me you've met him."

"Yes." We lay beside her. "We walked around with Pink."

"What do you think of him?" Said Y.

"How do you know him?"

Y turned on her side towards us. "Just like I know you. Through friends."

"Through Pink?"

"Yeah. Sort of."

"He knew where she was living." We said.

"Yeah, I don't really know how they've met. But he's okay." Said Y. "Like you."

She'll be surprised.

You too.

"He's even older than me." We told her.

We are ancient.

"A little." Said Y.

"Do you have any friends your age?" We said.

"People my age are boring." Said Y. "Even my ex is your age."

Well, she was something, wasn't she?

She looked at her phone again and started typing.

"What now?" We said.

"Lucas and I are talking."

"Oh, he doesn't give up." We put our hand on her belly.

Our hand travelled lower and lower. Y chuckled.

"He wants me to come over." She said.

"You can come over here too." We said as our hand reached her pussy.

It was moist and we started rubbing it, and Y began to moan.

"Come on." She moaned.

We watched as her eyelids fluttered and her mouth gaped.

"Let me... answer him." She said as the phone slipped to the floor.

Y looked at us and breathed heavily, and her hand was holding ours in an attempt to stop it. But we were in control and we pushed the tip of a finger inside her, and she moaned again. Y moved her lips as if she wanted to say something, but it didn't matter.

All that mattered was her hot, wet pussy.

When we were both done it was shower time. A huge cockroach was staring at our dick, so we got out to get a flip flop. Y laughed. She knew the drill.

"Let's go out. They'll be there." She said.

"Don't you have school tomorrow?"

"Our teacher's sick." Said Y.

"Is that what you tell your parents, too?"

She chuckled. We were funny, apparently.

"I don't tell my parents anything." She said. "As long as I have good grades, they don't care."

"Good for you, then. You're free." We said.

She was a small town girl and she was a total stranger to this city, and to its culture. She was a total stranger to us, and it's the thing we regret most on this Earth. Y was going to school because she had too, it was important to her parents, but the rest of her time she spent on buses to Tel Aviv and with her older friends.

We looked at her as we walked, holding our hand, enjoying her new life.

We gave her freedom.

"Are you sure they'll let you in?" We said.

"Of course they will. As long as I don't drink." She said. "The entrance is allowed. And you told me so much about this place."

"You'll meet all the crazy people. But good crazy."

We were thinking of the Under.Ground beasts. Bad crazy.

"Obviously." Said Y and shrugged. "Where else can we meet people?"

"At the café?"

"You were sitting and drinking nothing but beer, there too." Said Y.

"You've got a point." We said.

The Blue Bar was open and we went up the stairs and into the dark room. The regular singer was already on stage, tuning his guitar.

Not long after we sat, Pink and Lucas came in. When Pink hugged us we could feel her warm body, and an urge to do something. Lucas was looking around like a red eyed pigeon.

"Too bad they don't have anything vegan." He said.

He's already been there, apparently. Well, we weren't the only ones wandering at nights and finding hidden spots. The singer began screaming on stage.

"Oh." Said Y. "So that's his style."

"Yes." We said.

The sofa was attached to the wall, and Y and Pink were sitting on both of our sides. Lucas was the only one sitting in a chair, looking at the stage, and sometimes at Y. we put our hands around them both.

"Oh, come on." Said Pink and rolled her eyes at us.

Everyone was drinking except for Y, so we let her have some of our whiskey. Everything was normal for a while.

Then Lucas started talking about writing.

Tell us, do we sound like that, too?

"I write mostly short stories." He told us, but his eyes were staring at our hand around Y's shoulder. "People call it fiction, but it really isn't. I mean, maybe it's fiction in your head but once you put it on paper it's totally real."

"What do you mean 'totally real'?" Said Pink.

"I mean... it's like it actually happened." Said Lucas. "Somewhere."

We didn't listen to the music anymore. Now we stared at Lucas and listened carefully to our own ideas, coming out of his mouth. He said imagination is a part of reality, so what you can imagine, must be real. Writing it is like connecting the world of ideas to this world. And all that.

"And of course, it can also influence this world." Said Lucas.

We looked at Y sometimes just so he won't realize we're listening. For some reason, we didn't feel good about the fact that he agrees with us. It made our stomach twitch.

Our theory was, you can change your own life through writing, and also the lives of others. This isn't about creating stuff out of thin air, or about pulling a rabbit out of a hat.

Yes, you can preserve yourself after Death.

We and Lucas already talked about it.

Abracadabra was a word originally written on talismans throughout history to protect people from evil. It can be spoken as well, but with one major flaw: when spoken, it's temporary. When written, the magic word becomes eternal. The talismans could survive throughout the ages and reach people all over the world.

Lucas knew all that. We were sure of it, but we didn't know how. He finished his explanation and sat there like a ghost, curling a strand of hair around his finger.

We didn't like hearing our ideas spilling out from someone else.

And when we stood outside, we looked at him like he was prey.

"We're going to your place, right?" Y approached us.

"Yes." We said.

We hugged Pink and shook Lucas's hand. He was scratching his hair, slouching, just standing there. He was a weird creature in the night.

And when Y decided to go with us he bit his lower lip and looked away.

"Let's walk." We said.

Y was happy that night.

Too bad it ended the way it did.

"I didn't think Lucas has such theories about writing." We told her.

It was more than we expected.

Y shrugged. "He just likes it, I guess."

On our way we found a grassy slope, the edge of a small park in the middle of the city, between the high buildings and the busy roads. We ran to the top while Y stayed on the sidewalk.

But we just looked at her until she came up, and we both sat there looking at the stars.

We were on a desert island away from this place.

That night with Y was another world. We were another too. Free of these unending uniforms and of the need to be decent, smile and nod at the guests and sink our hands in their trash. In the dining hall, whether it's the guests or the workers, we had to wear our quiet face and be nice and thoughtful.

But with Y we could roll and mess around in the grass under the sky, even though she was too embarrassed and tried to stop us.

"The people!" She said.

"Who cares?"

She fell back laughing, but stopped to look at us when we leaned over her.

Those brown, dark eyes.

"You didn't like it when Lucas talked about writing."

"I don't like it when anybody talks about writing."

We don't like it at all.

"So how do you learn it? Do you just write?"

"I read a lot. And I see what other writers did." We said.

"Can you tell me?"

"About what?"

"About what they did."

"Oh. They were all travelers and nomads, drug and sex addicts."

Her mouth opened.

"Are you interested?" We said.

"People can't live too long like that."

"No, they can't."

Death never sleeps.

And so did we, that night in the cell. Y didn't want us to touch her in a public space, when all the stars are watching, so we went down to the street and got on the public minibus.

We couldn't see any of the faces, and we had to sit apart from Y. People at the back were transferring money to the passengers at the front, so they can pay the driver for them. We paid for ourselves, and Y paid for herself. Now it was time to wait, and we let the whiskey spin our thoughts.

Y was talking with someone at the back for the whole ride.

We were looking as the orange and yellow lights of the streets passed by us. Tender drops landed on the window and smeared the colors outside like crayons. A rainbow of possibilities.

Now we could do anything to this world.

You'll feel it too.

We came to this city alone, and we still felt alone even though things were a little different now. But we also knew we could disappear the next morning and no one would even notice. Pay attention, we were chasing eternal life as king. We were chasing, and Death was next to us, touching our thigh.

It was the only thing important. Everything else was expendable.

And yet, that night we only felt like lying in bed with her.

We told the driver where to stop and got out. Y came right after us, and we were making our way on the short walkway between the trees.

"What were you two blabbering about back there?" We said.

"Oh, he just asked why are you not paying for me, and I said you shouldn't pay, and he asked if we're together so I said yes and he asked again why didn't you pay and I told him you don't have to." Said Y.

"He said what?"

We stopped and turned around to look at her. Y was standing there in the circle of white light cast by the lamplight on the walkway to the building. She looked like a lost runaway child.

"He asked if we're together, and I said yes so he asked why you don't pay for me."

"No, before that." We told her.

"He asked if we're together." She said.

"And what did you say?"

"I said yes." Said Y.

We turned around and entered the building, and Y hurried behind us.

Half an hour later we were lying in the dark and listening to the roaches in the walls. We killed one as we entered the room. Y was beside us and her body was warm and soft, and our hands caressed her hair and neck.

We were surrounded by cockroaches bigger than your head. They were walking everywhere as if they were the owners. Our bed was a desert island between them, where we could hold her and believe she was real.

That night, sleep evaded us as Y hugged us in bed.

N is out there.

And maybe we really are not in control as much as we thought.

The last rain of the winter rattled outside, and the night was shining still.

CHAPTER XI

~

PUFF

We never saw Puff again.

But the last time was at the spice shop, and the scents closed on us like golden fingers, dragging us deeper and deeper. We wanted no one there, and no one came. The scents were fire-flies, filling the room with dull lights.

The room was full of blue smoke and our nostrils were tingling. The yellow light emphasized her natural tan, and her golden neck-lace and septum were shining like whiskey in a glass.

On the one hand, we wanted to listen. On the other hand, we couldn't help but feel the urge to tear her apart.

Puff hugged us, then moved back to inspect us with a smile. "Is that a gun in your pocket or are you just happy to see me?"

What was in our pocket?

We took it out and unfolded it. It was a cardboard coaster, the one we picked up at the Under.Ground. It's been a week, maybe two. We couldn't sleep.

"Huh." We tossed the coaster at Puff, and she caught it.

"What?" Said Puff.

"What does it say?"

"Tuborg."

"The other thing."

"Are you high?" She looked at her joint. "Well, you are. But it's just a coaster. Are you excited about stealing coasters from bars now?"

She tossed it on the counter.

We will kill you. N.

We put our finger there. "Look."

Puff leaned over the coaster. Her sleeveless cloth dropped a little. There was darkness there.

"What?"

"The writing."

Puff stood straight and crossed her arms on her chest. "It's a coaster!"

We held it up.

We will kill you. N.

"You say you dream of water a lot." She said.

Puff was an expert in dream interpretation, especially when she smoked.

Which was all the time.

"Yes." We said.

That's why we came to her. Our visions.

"Okay. So first of all, it's not like you can interpret all dreams through the same system." Said Puff. "It depends on how the dreamer feels about it. Understand? There are several guidelines, though. Like, water represents feelings."

We wanted to spread her legs and make her scream.

"But it's not just water. You say you dream of floods."

"Yes." We said.

"It means you're very emotional." Said Puff. "Even if you don't realize that."

We wondered how tight she would be down there.

"How can I not realize that?" We said.

"Maybe you're detached from yourself, honey." Said Puff as she sat down on her chair. "Or you don't let it out."

We wanted to let everything out.

"You need to be more in tune with yourself." She said and put out her joint.

Which one of us, Puff?

"You have to start thinking about it. How to be connected to yourself." She said. "Do you do that?"

"I write."

"You think it helps?" She examined us with her eyes, like a witch doctor.

"I notice things more. Internally. Like, the dreams."

"You don't sleep well, baby. I can see it in your eyes." Puff laughed. "You know what they say? It means someone else is dreaming about you, maybe."

Was it her?

She wasn't N.

"What does that mean?"

Puff looked at us. Her lips were bright red.

"It means you're possessed, honey."

We had a feeling about that.

But we had too much on our mind.

"Your internal dialogue won't let you sleep." Said Puff. "Stop it. Get in tune with yourself. I can help you with advice, but it's up to you."

We are many.

"Try and let it out a little. You know, start small. Cry sometimes."

We are King.

"Let your anger out, too. It's never good to keep things inside. It'll ruin your sleep... oh, well, it already has."

Her eyes pierced us. We couldn't, and didn't want, to escape.

"Show me your back tattoo."

"Sure." Puff turned around, lifting her tank top.

We saw the whole painting.

It was a winged woman crouching, with one foot on top a pile of books.

"What do you think?"

She rolled her tank top down and turned back to us.

"Why that?" Said we.

"She's a keeper of books." Puff shrugged. "I love losing myself in them. And in all kinds of other stuff."

What are you running from, little girl?

The urge to eat her there was almost consuming.

But her scents and eyes held us in place. Witch doctor.

She was okay.

Are we angry?

Not at all.

We are furious.

"What about N?" She said. "Do you still get messages?"

It was in our pocket.

She couldn't even see it.

"All the time." We said.

"Maybe it's someone you know." Her eyes became bright. "Maybe it's a lover!"

"I don't have any lovers."

"Well, you really don't." She laughed. "Every girl is just an-other hole in your belt, baby."

We looked at her.

"Try and think about people you know." Said Puff.

"I don't know anyone whose name starts with N."

"It's not about a name. Think of... who wants to talk to you, but can't." Puff shrugged. "I dunno. It's just my opinion. If you ask me, they're just street art or something."

"So you're not sure."

"Of course not, honey. I can't be sure of anything." Said Puff and lit a new joint. "I'm barely sure I'm even here."

The fire glowed orange as her tan, and it ran down the paper and hashish crumbs. It moved like a fairy eating away the stick, making its way to Puff's ringed fingers.

We fucked her once, just so you know.

She was screaming.

"Don't take it all too seriously." Said Puff.

We promised.

When we got out we had to breathe. The night was dark and the streets were orange, and Puff was one of several girls we found in the nights of Tel Aviv. But we didn't know what to do with them, so we let our hands work and said nothing.

Just like with Y, who was lying in our bed time after time and swallowed everything we gave her.

Still, we said nothing.

Home was far away.

CHAPTER XII

~

N WAS EVERYWHERE

N was everywhere.

All those inscriptions were not there to amuse us, we were sure of it. It was someone who knew, or thought that he knows, what we are doing. He knew why we came to this city, what we need to sacrifice, and he wasn't too pleased about it.

"We will kill you" was a hard promise to forget.

Pay attention now. Winter was coming to an end, and it was almost springtime. We were eating outside too much, drinking too much, living too much. Death reminded us of that. We had no old friends, just old strangers and new strangers. Since our arrival to Tel Aviv, we didn't stay in touch with anyone who was there when we first landed. So for Y and her friends we were a constant. Someone who was always there.

We only had our notebooks and our hole in the wall.

We sat at a café one night, Y, Lucas and us. He took the leftovers that someone left on the table and ate them. Lucas was a strange animal. He only ate vegan and he ate from dumpsters sometimes, because he didn't believe in spending money even though he had enough of it. We had none, and we were very into spending.

Some people are weirder than you can imagine.

Y accepted all this, even though she stopped eating his salads when we told her the vegetables come from the trash. She accepted everything, open to this new world that we all found in the streets of Tel Aviv at night.

She used to walk with us a lot.

We'd walk at daytime and we'd walk at nighttime. Sometimes when we went outside to eat, always a pizza or a burger, she would just sit there and keep us company. Once we even crowded together inside the small shower in the cell, we were both drinking the entire day and she was laughing...

And her laughter was water echoing from the tiles around us, like a whirlpool. She used to drink a lot and she used to laugh a lot.

Too bad it had to end this way.

And one night, after pizza, we walked with her to the bus stop. She was going to sleep at Lucas's.

"Don't you prefer staying?" Said we.

"Yeah. But Lucas needs me." Said Y.

"Can't he find someone else to eat his dumpster salads?"

Y chuckled. "No. He just... can't be alone. He's stressed at nights."

"Why?"

"I dunno." She shrugged. "But I have to be there to take care of him."

This guy was older and couldn't take care of himself. We already knew he wants her. We never asked if she complied.

"You're not his caretaker." We said. "Sleeping at a friend's is one thing, but being in charge of an unstable person is another."

"It's not like I have a choice." Said Y.

Through the haze of beer the air was cool and the tree leaves were rattling like tinfoil.

"What do you mean?" We said. "Tell him you're busy."

She was messing with her phone the whole time. We knew it was him. Writing to her, tempting her with Words.

"Never mind." Said Y. "He's just... he has some problems."

"Yes, I know."

"He can kill himself." She looked at us.

"Who told you that?"

We turned left on the main street.

"He did." Said Y, still texting.

We looked, but she moved the phone away.

We caught a glimpse, though. It didn't appear to be Lucas at all.

"Who's Night?" We said.

"That's his online name, that's how we met at first." Said Y. "It took me a while to start calling him Lucas."

Is that the official version, little girl?

"Well, he can call himself whatever he wants." We said. "But he can't tell you that he's going to kill himself if you are not there."

"He's depressed." She said.

It was not yet midnight, but not far from it. We were the only ones at the bus stop and we were waiting. Y was fourteen and she took care of everything everyone needed. She couldn't let us be alone, and she couldn't let Lucas be alone.

She took the call.

"Yeah, I'm waiting for the bus." She said into her phone.

We hated him then. The more she talked, the more we hated him. He had his own place in south Tel Aviv, and he had food and money. He's older than our body. All of these are fine. But pressuring her to come over through the phone, with threats of suicide, when he has all those things...

Y was too nice for any of us. And when we saw the tears in her eyes, as he begged her to come over, we realized.

"You shouldn't talk to him if he's making you cry." We said.

"It's okay." Said Y.

"Come on, hang up." We said and touched her shoulder.

Y was short and chubby and her eyes were wet. She really did care for him, and she really was afraid that he'll hurt himself. It wasn't the first time.

Do you know how many times he used that to make her come over? Or what else he asked her to do, if she doesn't want to be the one responsible?

Do you know? We neither.

But he was getting to her and her eyes were wet, and that's why we asked her to end that call. We asked again and again, but she couldn't. He was whispering in her ear.

Sometimes a good heart can bring you only sorrow.

"You're hurting me." We heard her say.

And as we looked, we were the ones holding her cellphone hand, squeezing tight.

"You should hang up." We said.

Her tears fell on her cheeks and into us. A drop hit the water in the dark. We looked at our hand that was gripping her, angry.

"Hang up the call." We said. "You can't agree to that."

Y looked at us with wet eyes. We had to let her go. She finished the call and then just stood there, quiet. She was such an idiot to bring herself into this situation, into his threats, and into our hands. We wanted to hug her and never let go, but our hands were not meant for that that night. They were angry hands. Vicious hands.

We waited with her until she got on the bus, and she looked at us through the window.

Believe us, we never meant to hurt her. We just wanted to hold her tight.

Life can put you in places you don't want to be in, make you do things you shouldn't, and make you look very different than what you are. But we are that, and we are not that. We are many.

And we are Monster.

We sat at the bus station, waiting for nothing.

The stars were visible and we stared back at them. The wind was a soft maiden's hair and the Earth was flat from beginning to end, so we could walk to its edge and one step further. We got up and walked.

The Blue Bar was open.

We went to the restroom. Not to pee, just to check.

Do not interfere. N.

Thanks a lot. We'll remember that.

Blondy nodded at us, and we saw Pink in the corner. We found a plaything for the night, and whiskey.

"What are you doing here?" We said.

"Are you mad?" She said.

"Not at all."

"I just ran away from home."

We looked at her.

"I mean, it was just an argument. So I came here. I didn't really run, all my stuff is there." She said. "I still had this book in my bag. Maybe you'll like it."

She handed us a weird one.

Its title said Open me.

The upper margin said, Do not interfere. N.

We heard you the first time.

We closed the book and brushed our hand in hers when we gave it to her.

Pink and we started drinking. The music was new, black polished chrome, and we were beginning to change. Pink was looking at us, but she looked away when we looked back. She looked like she was looking for something.

When the regular singer finished he asked if anyone else want to go on.

"Maybe you should." Said Pink.

"Maybe you should." We retorted.

Her pink lips smiled.

And our legs lifted us and walked towards the stage.

Singer looked at us. "Do you need music? Anything?"

Our legs got up on stage, and our eyes peered into him.

"Yes."

He started playing his guitar again and the music was a living jungle of lizards circling us, taking us away, moving our body in angles we didn't mean to. We were on stage with the music, because we had no choice. We took off our shirt, and Pink got up.

She could see our ribs.

Our bones.

Sleepless.

Then our mouth opened.

It was Death speaking, a monster, something we couldn't control or reason with. We found out that we are mad.

We are furious.

The words were accumulating to a storm. We were almost there. On the verge of it. Looking straight into the abyss. Getting ready to jump.

And the Words stopped.

Premature ejaculation.

The music was orange, electric tinfoil, and Singer looked at us. So did everyone else. Our eyes went straight to Pink's neck, hidden beneath her brown hair. Death whispered in our ear, and we smiled.

"Are you okay?" She said.

We put on our shirt. "I'll get back to you."

And as we looked at the stickers on the walls, one was calling us.

Do not interfere. N.

"Let's get out of here." We told Pink.

And as we walked out she said, "I really liked how your poem got intense all of a sudden and then became softer."

Was it a poem? Or a howl?

We couldn't remember a single word of it.

Makes sense, we weren't the ones talking.

We wanted to drag Pink somewhere and throw her into the abyss.

And when our lips touched at the bus stop, we could taste fear.

Our hand gripped her breasts under her shirt. Our cock was hard.

"Stop."

We wanted her.

"Come on."

Not her body.

"Come on, please." She said. "We're in the middle of the street."

We wanted her soul.

We wanted Y's soul.

A young, innocent soul. It was raw, tender, something to devour.

"I'm going home." Said Pink as if she wanted to leave before she'll do anything she'll regret about. As if she hasn't already done.

"What about running away? You can come sleep at my place." We said.

"No, it's okay, thanks. It was just an argument." She said. "I should get back."

Her eyes were staring at the sidewalk, and she stayed that way until the bus came. Our hand was on hers, and we almost didn't let go. We kissed her hard before she disappeared inside the bus, staring at us with sad, desperate eyes.

Pink wanted nothing to do with us.

She was too afraid of her urges.

We were not.

TRANSMOGRIFICATION

CHAPTER I

THE LIZARD KING

It was a disaster waiting to happen.

Y's parents were away. She told us they're on vacation abroad, and she has the whole house to herself. We were planning on watching a movie and drinking a lot, and we were saving every coin from our hotel tips, for the bus and the movie renting.

"What's bothering you?" We said.

Y looked up from her phone. We were sitting at a café, starving. The sun flew in through the display window, and the people outside were riding skates or walking their dogs or whatever it is that people do to pass time.

"Lucas had an alcohol poisoning." Said Y.

"He should drink less, then."

"He says it helps him write." She shrugged.

Sounds familiar.

Alcohol unleashes the beast in the body. Not only the ability to act, but also the ability to hold a pen forever and write write write, until your muscles are sore. Until everything else fades and the people are slaughtered, and there remains only paper and ink. It is essential for Inspiration, if you seek it.

Luckily, you aren't.

It is essential for writing the truth and acting the truth.

And it is essential for drowning your nightmares and routine.

We watched the sea from the hotel, and we watched Gideon and the pigeons and knives. Alcohol opens the cage for all the human safari, and all the fetish lovers and weirdoes come out. And we mixed with them to taste them, to make them eternal.

Alcohol and writing, both are good to research your head.

We tried to get as far away from ourselves as we can.

Lucas was a walking pile of fear and he was probably torturing himself, and so he also tried to run away. From what exactly, we couldn't tell. We could barely tell what we are running from, but we knew we were running, of course. Death told us that.

And so in our run we came across the little princess, and it happened to be feeding time. We knew we are going to have the house for ourselves there, in her little town that we've never been to. A whole place to do as we please.

She won't stand in our way.

It was the day, and we woke up that morning just like in any other morning. Y was there the night before, a wicked dream on the bed. She was between our thighs again and her teeth and tongue were fire in our loins. We fell asleep not long after we were emptied into her, and she swallowed it and came to lie beside us.

But that morning she was gone, and we got up to see our messy face in the mirror. This isn't a dream. It's just summer. We slept naked and still we were sweaty, and drops of thick water were running down our nose. Dry, hot wind came in through the open window.

We had to shed off our skin.

Then we noticed a loaf of bread on the table. There was a yellow, wrinkled note under it. We picked up the note first, and we couldn't move much, but just stand there staring at the words. We were fixated to this message.

"I had to leave early. I'll be home. In the meantime I bought you some bread because you ran out of food. Come and see me. You can take bus line number 500. And please don't forget to bring the movie we wanted to see. I'm waiting. See you. Y."

It was her round handwriting in blue pen. And it was beautiful. At first we just stood there and held it and let the sun caress our naked body. Then we couldn't stand anymore so we just sat on the bed and looked at the bread on the table, and our heart and stomach shrunk until they were nothing at all.

We felt like crying.

Well, you should know we've known several girls by then. None of them were as gentle, as caring, as Y. None of them was willing to do such things for us, and so, we didn't know what to think of it. We just sat there and again saw our face in the mirror.

We shouldn't go. She doesn't deserve this.

Then again, we had to go. Say "yes", and ye shall be redeemed.

And so we let the water in the shower wash away the night and wore a long, black pair of pants, and a white shirt, and our leather shoes and leather belt, adorned with silver snake scales. We took our shoulder bag full of secret notebooks and closed the window, for we knew we are not coming back that night. We went out to the outer part between the doors, and it was dark and small. We never saw who's behind the other door, and we simply went out of the cave and left the building straight to the street.

It was as hot as you can imagine. The people were out and women were wearing their body parts outside their clothes. If there's one thing that can make a beast out of you, it's that rising urge inside.

Today we are going to leave this city for the first time in almost eight months. We'll see the world outside, and we'll bring ours with us.

The video rental place was in the record store in front of the mall, and so we decided to visit Puff first.

The clerk at the spice shop looked at us.

"How can I help you?" He smiled.

"Is Puff around?"

"Oh." Said Clerk. He was tall and tanned.

They're all tanned and orange in this city.

"She won't be around anymore." He said. "She left."

"Left where?"

He shrugged. "That's all I know. She said she's leaving the city."

Seems like everybody's leaving the city. They come to play here in those streets and then they're tired of it, and they have to run away. But the city is all consuming and its streety tentacles reach everywhere once you touch them once. We touched them many times.

And to prove us right, an inscription written with a marker pen on a lamplight post, said:

It's everywhere. N.

We got the movie and started walking to one of Tel Aviv's main bus stations. As we walked, the sun was pure white and told us of magic rituals, of people getting obscene and dance around the fire

115

through the ages. Some of them just happen to only have an internal fire... and they go from generation to generation, possessing and possessed, transferring their traditions onward.

Puff was very into this, and she kept talking of shamans connecting this world and others. They were loners who talked to the wind, and they were birds of prey and cobras and leopards. Complete chaos and disorder in their souls, they were open to host others. Puff believed that if she'd take acid she'll be possessed. We believed it happens through alcohol and writing. Puff said anything can do it, but you need to have a very open mind.

When you think of possession you think of ghosts floating mid-air and diving into people's bodies. But that's not it. Everything you are is stored in your mind, and if we study your mind long enough and adopt your habits, we are possessed. So far we kept it low key, but that night we meant to go for it. Even if it would end with our death, that's okay.

Death is only a small price to pay for immortality.

The bus station was right next to the central railway station. We worried a bit about missing the bus, but it appeared right in front of us while we were conversing with the sun. The sign on the windshield said "500".

At first we saw Do not interfere. N., but when we looked again we realized we were wrong.

It said 500.

"When are you leaving?" We said.

The driver was a fat, tired man, sweating in his uniforms. Armpit sweat stains were visible on his white shirt. His white moustache matched it.

116

"Ten minutes." He said.

We took out our change. It was either a pizza, or riding this bus to Y's empty castle. We couldn't afford both. And we didn't have to, either.

He gave us a ticket and we sat a few seats behind him. Death sat beside us and we were glad for it, because this means no other people would sit there. We were by ourselves and we wanted to be by ourselves. We wanted to watch a movie and drink a lot and fuck whoever we can find. Y.

And then the engine hummed and the bus started moving. The sun was still steady in the sky though, a radiant, cool, jewel of an eye. Soon Tel Aviv will be gone, and the abyss will be open.

Beware now.

If you have any sensitivity as to the fate of fourteen year old girls who are locked in an empty house with a man who deals with possessions, go no further. This is by no means a narrative trick, but a fair warning.

For our ritual of possession was successful.

CHAPTER II

~

A WARM MANSION

The small town was quiet and uneventful. The sky was pure blue and the trees were silently moving, and the world was but a dream. And every dream has an end.

We arrived at the address she gave us and Y stepped outside. It was a big house. We mean a real house. A house with a front, with windows and a tiled, faded red roof. On the inside was furniture. To our left was a living room, with a sofa and a TV and pictures on the walls. Then there was the kitchen, with an oven and a fridge and a gas cooker, and to our right were stairs. Stairs going up and stairs going down, and we couldn't see what's in there. It was a warm mansion.

Y was a beautiful princess then, dressed in a too big, white shirt, and her golden curls rested on her shoulders. She was barefoot as a saint and she wrapped her arms around us, and it reminded us of the bread and all of the rest.

"What's up there?" We said.

"My room and my parents' room." Said Y in a quiet voice.

They had lots of rooms. We only had one. A dirty hole in the wall.

That house was spotless and all drenched in white. The floor reflected the sun and our blurry figures on the big, square tiles.

"What's down there?" We said.

"Just a TV room." Y shrugged. "We have too many rooms."

They did.

"How's Lucas?" We said.

"Oh, he's fine now." Said Y. "He drank too much, he collapsed, and he recovered at the hospital."

"Did you visit?"

"No." Said Y. "I visited him at home."

"Is it big like this one?"

We looked up to the high ceiling.

Y chuckled. "No. it's just an apartment. Are you okay?"

"Yes."

"How was your ride?" She said.

"Not many people come here."

"Not during the day." Y chuckled again. "People come back from work later, or they leave in the morning."

The ride lasted about an hour, and besides us there were just a group of teenagers and several old people. The kids were noisy as expected, as kids always are.

Y is a teenager, we reminded ourselves.

And we were ancient.

Possession in our body.

"I'm glad you got off on the right stop, at least." Said Y.

"Didn't you say Pink lives here too?" We said.

"Oh," Said Y. "she lives just next door. She'll come tonight."

"Oh, so you really do know each other." We said. "For a long time."

"Yep." Y smiled. "Let's go up."

We followed her up the stairs. When she came to us we had nothing to offer, the cell was really small, and even though Y kept asking for permission to come she didn't really have to. It was just us. However, this was her parents' home and it felt like it. It was big and we didn't know what's in it, and we had to let her lead.

At least for a while.

The upper floor contained the washroom, complete with a bath and a toilet. Then there was her room, and her parents' room which was on the other side of the floor, and closed. We wondered what we might find in there but we didn't dare checking.

You should know by now, we were a bit scared of the place.

Y's room was rather small and contained mostly her big bed, a closet and a window. The walls were a shade of purplish blue.

It was very different from Moon's room, all messy and wild with the glass broken due to fits of rage, and it was different than the bookstore and The Blue Bar. It was just a room, the room you might find when dealing with a normal fourteen year old girl.

We felt very out of place.

That girl was sucking our cock at nights.

"Oh, I forgot." Said Y. "Do you want anything to drink?"

"You mean beer?" We looked at her.

"Of course." She chuckled.

She knows us. At least a part of us. And so we went back downstairs and got two bottles of beer out, and went back to her room. Y waited with her drink until we got there, but we already started on the way.

"So what do you do here all the time?" We said.

"Nothing much. I go out, or I read, or whatever." Said Y. "I'm looking for acting schools."

"You'll be a great actress." We said.

Y laughed and almost choked on her beer. "You don't know that."

"I know everything." We said.

We looked at her sitting there on the bed, her back to the wall by the window, her knees folded to her chest.

"I'll write parts for you." We said.

"Did you ever write a play?"

"I have. I wrote everything you can imagine."

You have to write everything you can imagine and you can't limit yourself to one type of work and say "that's what I'm going to do", because that way you can't mix things and you eventually limit your own self-expression. How can you create a world without self-expression?

However, you never become that. You are born that. Or you are being possessed to achieve that.

So, wouldn't you go for it?

But we didn't even know if we were a poet, or something entirely different.

As you probably noticed.

"So how many notebooks do you have?" Said Y.

"I don't even know." Said we. "I just write them."

"Nothing specific?"

We shrugged. "It's not very structured yet."

Our mission would never be complete.

We got on the bed and crawled towards her. Y put the bottle between her folded legs. She raised her eyes at us.

"I really want to read it already." She said.

"You'll like it." We said without a smile.

"I know."

We leaned forward and kissed her forehead and our hands cupped her cheeks.

"Wanna see something cool?" Said Y.

"Sure." We said.

She turned to the window and opened it. There was a window screen behind the glass, and Y opened that too. Then she got out to the roof and started walking on the tiles.

"What are you doing?" We said.

Y was a weightless cat walking on the clouds, among a thousand invisible birds. We heard them on the trees below us, in the yard. The neighboring house was quite far. We were above the streets, in our own little piece of azure.

We could take the whole house and fly with it around the world.

"Come back in." We said.

"Don't you wanna come outside?" Said Y.

"Not right now." We said.

And so she came back in and closed the window, and we began our drinking party. There was still light outside when we started drinking. We had to break free of our chains. We started with the beer but Y had access to her parents' drinks too, and so when we decided to watch the movie we were already pretty open.

The crowd arrived just in time for the screening. They were Y's local friends. We were tingling. One was a skinny, bespectacled guy. And a little girl dressed in purple, slick black hair, smooth as raven's claws. You get the picture.

This was Pink's little sister, Y's friend from school.

We smiled at her.

She smiled back.

And Pink entered, smiling but not looking straight at us. She was alone, as usual, and she remembered us to well. Maybe she'll be chosen tonight for the ritual. Maybe someone else.

We all were drinking and we all went down into the TV room. We all watched the screen getting bigger and bigger with moving figures. They were possessed. Talking, screaming, playing music.

And so that part of the ritual started.

Pay attention.

We allowed the music into our bones and danced with it. The notes were hungry spirits looking for a soul to take. We were just the vessel, that's what we prepared ourselves for. And the music swirled and swirled. We were downstairs, in the TV room, which was a dark Indian cave that fit us perfectly. The music was electric and we were moving, and the room was full of shadows and shapes of white light.

We let them take our body, move it, jump with it. We mean to say, we were getting out. The chains were weak, and the body was almost ours. We were King, and we could do anything. We felt ourselves change into something else.

People were backing away from our presence. They were looking, frozen. Now they will know us. All of them. Now they will see, and they will never forget.

An insatiable hunger consumed us. And this girl, the new one, was standing in the corner, eyes wide open, a deer in the headlights.

She was Pink's sister.

We wanted blood.

We moved this piece of flesh and we felt every muscle tensing, and the room was spots of light and shadow. We wanted to spread her legs and just get inside, and eat that little girl alive.

Take her to a place from which there is no return. To any of us.

We were hungry for blood and sex. Nothing more than that.

No, there was something more.

We wanted her to shake in fear.

We wanted her to fear us.

And she should, for we are Beast, and we destroy. And as we approached her she was pierced, and she stood there pale and small. Then she saw it, we're sure of it. She saw what we see.

She saw Death.

We looked into her eyes, and Death smiled.

We were almost there.

Take her with us. Tear her apart. Make her eternal.

We are King.

A lightning bolt rattled this body and we lost control of it. We were a spirit of vengeance, we were rage in flesh form. And we were falling.

The floor hit us, and we lay on our side. The hands and legs moved and we could only watch them, and we felt the chains wrapping around us again, and we were about to be dragged back into the cage. The music was endless. The TV cast shapes all around us.

And the whiskey just spilled out with all the spirits.

It was radiant yellow and it spread on the floor. We were a snake in a pool of whiskey. And we screeched as the fluids flew out and as the body twitched. We fought it. We fought the chains.

Death crouched in front of us and hid her legs behind him. He was ready, he could have done it, he could have taken us already.

Unfortunately, believe us when we say it, we stayed here.

Abandoned.

And we were so close to spreading her legs, to destroying her right there. To taking her to a place from which she could never return, from which we didn't want her to return. A place where we have full control, and she has none. Lying on her back, crying and screaming.

We stretched out our hand towards her.

More whiskey came out.

And the music was over.

CHAPTER III

～

TRANSMOGRIFIED

The world was nowhere to be found.

Flashes of light were dancing midair, pointing and laughing. We heard a voice and there was movement on the floor, and the walls were spinning.

Then we were out.

The white lights shined on the floor tiles brighter than midday, and they were carrying the body. It used to be ours. Glasses was holding the armpits while Y was carrying the legs.

"To the bath." She said.

The white shirt was all stained with brown yellow fluids.

We were again a lizard on the wall, and we remember watching as they carried the twitching figure. We were transmogrified. Y and Glasses were carrying the body upstairs and we followed, for we couldn't avoid it to stay downstairs and rip that girl in half through her loins. The stairs curved right and they could barely hold the dead body, twitching silently. They dropped it in the bath, and Y said:

"Take off his cloths."

And as Glasses pulled off the stained, wet shirt, she was going for the pants. The leather belt and shoes were off and the fly was opened. Y was getting more and more lost with every pull of the pants, until they were off. The body looked inhuman.

It's eyes were rolled and staring and it's body was full of red marks and swollen, green arteries, forearms scarred and the brown yellow acid flowing out the mouth like swamp mud spreading. Its fingers twitched and its knees bent.

No cloths, in the bath, total freedom.

We crapped in the bath while they were standing there, and we remember the dark brown lump coming out smoothly, like a big cockroach seeking his place.

"Oh no." Said Y. And she rushed outside and put her child hand in a nylon bag and caught the roach before he could get away with all of his evil load, and threw it in the toilet.

Our brave princess.

There was water. We couldn't feel them. In dreams, water is all your unsatisfied urges and your will to power. And we were flooded in that body and we couldn't get out again. The water was rising, transparent, thick, and the light was too heavy on the eyes.

The world was nowhere to be found. It was far, far away, a transient memory in the mind. It was a piece of azure being smothered in feces and puke. Bowel fluids. And it was a refugee child princess who was being forever stained.

Trust us, there is nothing we remember as vividly as this.

It was Death whom we found looking at us when the eyes were open. The walls were a purplish blue shade and the room was dark. We were staring at the ceiling, severed from the body, breathing in vain. We wanted to count our fingers but our hand did not cooperate. Well, this must be a dream anyway.

This can't be real.

Oh, but it is.

Death told us that.

And our limbs were twitching and there was nobody there. We tried remembering where we are or how did we get there. We tried remembering her hands touching this body, but we couldn't. We felt nothing, not on our skin and not inside it. Everything was a film, frame after frame, which we were watching in repeat. Not the hard floor, not the cold china, not the wetness of water. There was no pain and no sensation. Just changing images.

If our hands didn't sense it, it never happened. It was all inside of us, and we were the world we were looking for, for so long. We were Inspiration.

Our bowels moved.

Death told us that.

Somehow we were in the washroom, sitting on the toilet, staring at the bath. It looked dry and clean. The curtain was yellow. There was sunlight in the mirror over the sink and we sat too low to see the eyes. We crapped again, big chunks of brown, dead roach corpses. They were swarming out as the gate was opened. What a rush, they hurried in the water and the drains.

We were wrong to think that we shed our skin and moved on. It was our skin that shed us, and was left empty on the toilet, hunching, white nylon.

It really did happen.

Death told us that.

We screamed. We never screamed like that before. Our lungs were torn out of our chest, our mouth was a black horn and our body was fading. There was nothing but that scream. And in that scream there was a name.

We screamed her name.

We were fighting Death. And Y came in and she was a pale ghost angel and her eyes were wide open, and we couldn't even look at her. But we were fading.

"Water."

She ran out.

We screamed her name against Death. We screamed for her to come and save us. But redemption was no option then, and we were screaming as he held our bowels and our lungs and our heart. Death squeezed and smiled and Y couldn't even see him. She must have thought we were crazy when she came in, holding a big bottle of clear water. She must have known we're a monster. And she must have thanked God we can't get up, for we would have killed her if we could.

Kill them all.

Water was flowing down our throat. Y looked at our silent body, frozen, and we bent toward the bucket. It was our bucket. It was next to the bed. Now it was between our legs, and we puked a pale shade of transparent yellow. We didn't even notice if we crapped again or if we even breathed.

It all was rushing up and shooting out.

We knew we might die there on the toilet. She knew it too. And she knew that in our current state, it's either us or her. It's dying or killing. Either way, it is to haunt her forever.

We emptied the water bottle.

"More."

129

She took it and disappeared again, and again Death was pulling our organs and we screamed her name. We couldn't let her go far. She was our Death witness.

There was no was else in the world.

We are another.

We didn't act, but watched helplessly as it all took place within and through our body. It was a tool for other forces. It was nothing we could stop or deny, all the gates were open, and horror flowed outside. We drank another bottle. As we poured the water in our throat we felt it slithering down, cool, spreading through the blood and nerves.

We had no idea what our other openings were doing.

Y was sitting on a stool and looking at us. She seemed scared and we liked it, but she also seemed... disappointed. It was not as appealing as fear, trust us.

But she knew, as we wanted her to know, that she is in our hands there. She knew we are something to get rid of, or to be crushed by.

We are Monster.

"How did I get in bed?" Said the lips.

"Glasses and I took you there."

"Is he here?" Said the lips.

"No. They all left."

"When?" Said the lips.

"Last night. A little bit later."

Said the lips, "Only you stayed."

We were hunching over our knees, staring. We were full of water.

"What do you remember?" Said Y.

"Everything."

We knew it worked. It was a trance, a dance of influence, flesh and blood possessed.

She eventually left and we stayed there, because our body wouldn't move. Death was squeezing our stomach with his long fingers inside us. With each squeeze we felt the air coming out of our mouth, and fluids swirling. Our bucket was a third full.

We screamed her name.

Part the need part rage was rising in us like the tide, when the water is attracted to the moon. We were starving and dehydrated and we couldn't believe we'll survive that day. Not without her, at least.

And poor Y, she did the best she could. She made food and came to sit with us, asking again and again if we're okay. We were sure this is our last day in this body. We were absolute rage and vengeance, trapped in a weak, fragile, flesh form. And we had to change, but it was out of our hands.

There was something else inside of us.

Something older than this body and very deep, like water penetrating the rocks. Like a shadow. It made us say "yes" when we wanted to say "no". It made us go out when we wanted to sleep. And it made us write write write when we wanted to rest, and let our hands go free of that mission. We couldn't resist it.

That night we were engulfed by it.

Y was hopeless, sitting on the stool or wandering the house. When she sat there she looked at us as if she had just woken from a dream, and she knows it will never be the same. For us it didn't matter. We were almost dead.

Or we were dead already.

With no feeling at all in our body we got up. We had no idea how long we sat there, and as we got up, Y got up. However, she kept her distance. As we looked at her, she took a step back. Completely bare, she could see our arteries and scars and body hair, a beast, hunching, gritting teeth, a mask of rage and helplessness.

We got in the bath and turned on the water. As they touched us our knees bent, and we were at the bottom of the abyss. Y was there. And our memories are someone else's. We know not what happened later.

Y helped us get in bed and we lay there, and Death was poking his fingers in our guts, and we were screaming still. The door was closed. The world was empty, and we transitioned between sleep and wakefulness.

In a little dream she's an actress in a big, silent mansion, by herself day by day. She lives on a small island of azure at a world's end. We're a wanderer. Always have been. And so we knock on her door, sweaty and loaded with bags after one more long ride. A poet. A man wandering from word to word, from thought to thought, from place to place with no known destination. No responsibility. We knock on her door. She sits on the red tiles in the shadow of the solar water heater every day. She sometimes listens to the wind, staring at the clouds, wishing they would take her away. She slides off the roof gently like a weightless cat, made of nothing but dust. This house is now her playground. She dances in all the rooms. People next door are far away. We knock on her door. We're tired of another journey from the heart of the city to the end of the night. But this is her world now, and we are soft and weak and powerless. She's so small in that big, warm mansion.

We knock on her door.

And when the door opened we saw Y and we had nothing more to say. We've said it all in our dream, and we weren't sure it even ended. An empty shell, we lifted our head from the mattress.

"Are you asleep?"

We didn't know what to answer, so we just kept our mouth closed. But our body sat up.

"Dinner will be ready soon." She said.

"Okay." We whispered.

She was out and we noticed the room was full of soft darkness, and the sun was gone. Outside the birds were still chirping. One made a sound, and another answered. It went on back and forth. We managed to wear our black pants and started looking for a shirt.

Ours was not there. It was probably unusable.

Barefoot, we got another shirt out of our bag. We had hiccups all the way down the stairs that last night served as our bridge to ghostly torment.

Where was home?

"It's almost ready." Said Y. "It's in the oven."

We said nothing. We walked towards her with our body like a cloth in the wind, a staring snake, and she was frozen. Now we got our body back.

The radio was on and playing as she cooked and the music was a soft parade.

The trash bin was full of last night's leftovers, neon light spiders were crawling on the ceiling. We held her hand and then her waist, and the evening was a fading dream. To the sounds of radio music we slowly danced, slow, and we only listened to the hearts' beating, smelling dinner that was not yet ready. The evening changed into another picture in a wanderer's album, between the empty pages.

Not to touch the earth, we were floating midair. Not to see the sun, but exist transiently forgotten by all, in realms of light and bliss. The shadows of the trees were witnessing us through the windows, dancing in the breeze. Not to say a thing, for nothing we could say would have been fitting. Yes, we write. And still, sometimes words are not enough.

Y put her head on our chest, and then we knew, unfortunately, that we are still alive. And as the oven dinged she left us and took out the tray, and put it on the countertop. There was nothing there but roasted vegetables, and that's all we needed.

"You can't eat heavy stuff." Said Y as we sat.

We didn't even want anything else. At that point we wanted neither food nor water, and we barely even wanted to breathe. We wanted to get that ache away from our gut and fall asleep and wake for eternity in another world. We ate slowly and as we were both done, Y took us to her bed.

We were ancient. Falling apart.

Y and we lay on the bed in the dark and looked at the god figure on her closed door. The room was shrouded with hazy darkness. Our fingertips felt her warmth, finally. The sea was calm and flat and deep, and the water only moved in minor currents on the surface. We could dive inside together, no matter what we find in there. Take a journey to the depth of the abyss.

We didn't.

We stayed.

Are we another?

Instead we lay there, listening to her breathe. It was her world now. Food in the fridge, light, a real bed.

And nothing scratching at the walls.

Out there, there were trillions of stars. Out there we were new, immaculate.

CHAPTER IV

⌒

THE BREAKWATER

We were sitting on the breakwater one cool night, and The Mediterranean was a black abyss of unknown forces. This is where ancient gods were worshipped. There were no stars and the sea was one with the sky, a wedding of black. We could hear the waves bite the rocks beneath us and the whistle of the wind. We could float endlessly in that void and no one would find us.

We could jump, all it takes is one second, and then you swim to the sunken gardens.

We don't know how long it has been since the ritual. We don't even know if it worked. It seemed to backfire then, at Y's mansion of azure, and we were seeing those spirits every day. We were deep into summer now, hot and humid, and we were alone.

We are never alone.

But we felt as if the world has been taken away from us. Y took care of us, she had to. But we left and got back to the hole in the wall, to pass the time with ourselves.

How could it end that way?

Well, every end is a beginning.

We looked at the black abyss of water, and there were no re-flections. Maybe The Iguana is swimming down there, making bat-tle with The Worm. Something inside of us wanted to go there.

Something else inside of us, wanted Opportunity.

"How old are you?" We said.

"Twenty." Said Alice.

"Where did you go to school?"

"Tel Aviv." She chuckled.

Alice was dressed in black again and her green eyes were stars in space. The wind that was woven in her hair had dyed her cheeks with a shade of pink.

We were walking together all along the beach until this breakwater at the north of Tel Aviv. We barely visited that area, and it was foreign territory. But instead of investigating the streets we turned left, straight to the sea, and walked on the rocks into the water. Alice just walked beside us, barely touching us.

Pay attention.

We wanted to know if she can be a new beginning for us, for we knew that Y and we have no future in this city, or outside of it. Yes, we would have loved to get her in our bed, lay her down, spread her... well, these urges were still there. But we also had to get away from Y, and find someone else.

"What are your plans?" Said Alice. "You keep asking me about mine."

"I'll publish my book sometime soon." We said.

"And?"

"And what?"

If the tide will come, the sea will take us. We looked over at the unseen horizon, looking for some kind of light. A spark. A firefly.

Nothing.

Alice leaned backwards on her palms. Her shirt rounded around her breasts. We were leaning forward, looking at her and at the water. There was Magic in both directions. We just couldn't choose.

"I don't know. Being a writer." We said.

"What does being a writer mean?"

We will tell you the truth, we had no idea. We though it meant living, then dying. But for some reason, Death didn't take us that night, and we just kept on going.

"Can you make money off of it?" Said Alice.

"Well, even if you can't..." We said. "What does it matter?" We looked at her. "Do you prefer hating your job?"

Did you ever lay on your back and spread your legs for someone? We didn't say.

"Everyone can find a job they like." Said Alice. "I won't hate my job."

"Maybe you will." We said. "How do you know?"

Have you ever sucked so hard you could barely breathe? We didn't say.

"Maybe I will." She shrugged. "But I'm working on not hating it."

"Do you plan on making a career in your subject?" We said.

Have you ever kissed someone like you really mean it, and couldn't let him go? We didn't say.

"Yeah. Maybe in research." Said Alice. "What if you won't make it?"

"If you believe in yourself enough, and let it lead you, you'll make it." We said. "Are you worried about your future?"

Will you hug us just so we can feel your breaths and warmth, and hold our hand as we walk? We didn't say.

"Actually... I am." Said Alice. "Don't you?"

"Never." We said.

Will you have a future with us? We didn't say.

"Never?" She laughed.

This is what being a writer means, we suppose. Never.

We walked with her on the rocks back to shore. We didn't want to leave the sound and smell of water, but we did. We came to this city to find Inspiration, to experience different life and find adventures. Then we wanted to mix it all to a text that'll keep us alive forever in a world of our own creation.

Then we met Y. Y was fourteen. She had to go to school and listen to her parents, even though she didn't want to. No one would ever approve of this. We are seven years her senior.

Then we met Alice. She was closer to our age and she had plans for her future. It could include us. She was shy and embarrassed, and probably a virgin. She was someone we could go out with, without the interference of others. She was... normal.

However, as we walked to the bus stop, she didn't even touch us.

"Are you sure you don't want to sleep at my place?" We said.

"No, that's okay." Alice smiled. "I have a lot to do tomorrow."

When the bus arrived she almost didn't hug us, too, and we had to hug her as if she didn't know it was an accepted custom. It was a step back from last time, which she didn't mention in a word. Like it never happened, and we were nothing but friends and not two people who hold a shared secret.

We killed a cockroach as we entered our hole and masturbated just to get her out of our head. But truth was we were confused about it. She seemed uninterested. Maybe we didn't have a future after all, and we should find someone else or stick to the one who does show her interest...

This is why, that day, when the sun was shining outside the bookstore in the mall, we were left speechless. Alice came in and sat beside us as we were reading another Kerouac again.

Scribbled secret notebooks, and wild typewritten pages, for yr own joy.

Do not interfere. N.

"Are you dating Y?" Said Alice.

We know no one would like to hear this. But also, we didn't date Y. Even though she may have thought that we do.

"Are you?" Said Alice. She was dressed in grey now.

"Who told you that?" We said.

"She did. Yesterday, when I met her." Said Alice. "She told me you were dating."

"What did you say?"

"I said we are, too." Said Alice.

Trust us, we really didn't know what to say. First of all, because we're not fucking stupid. Obviously, if we want to mess around, we won't do it with two girls who are friends and who know each other, and have mutual friends who talk.

Alice got up and left and we just stayed there. What else could we do?

Who could we talk to?

Y came to sleep at our cell because she didn't want to sleep at her parents', and she needed a place to be. We only got out of there for walks, which usually concluded with us eating while she's watching and laughing, amused at how we could eat a whole tray of pizza by ourselves. She joined us twice at The Blue Bar, always with more friends, and once when we dragged her to that fetish party, which she didn't like at all.

None of it, as you know, is dating.

We didn't date Alice either. We had a sexual encounter on the street once, and the next time we saw her she showed no interest at all.

We also didn't date Moon, even though we fucked. And we didn't date Puff, whom we visited at work, or Pink, who had her boyfriend on her mind. We also didn't date Sally, even though we joined her cigarette breaks at the hotel.

Going to the movies, bringing flowers, taking a girl out... trust us, we were free of all that. And that's why we could do whatever we wanted.

Now you must know why we didn't say a thing. We weren't surprised. Well, they were friends. Obviously it wasn't a big secret. But we really weren't dating. If it sounds like our statement of defense, so be it.

And so not only Alice confused us on the weekend with her cold-warm behavior, now she was even more confusing. The only thing we could do was going home and drinking about it. We saw no point in talking to Y, and allowed her to make first contact. But we had an urge to dive deep in our brain and let it all out on paper.

Our visions became more and more frequent, more and more detailed. An opening inside us was torn by the bite of a wild beast. Now we had to accept everything that was coming.

But sometimes we wondered where is it going to. This chain of rapid visions racing in front of us day and night, slowly severing us from the outside world. Who's orchestrating this?

So we put pen to paper on our bed. We had no other choice.

We formed shapes and colors. Another world. And we wrote and we wrote, because like Alice said, we had to create our own future and live beyond Death that may come in the morning. And the words were flying until Dawn touched us with white fingers that colored all with a deep darkness. It was cold. We smelled the rocks of this land of nightmares. They were chasing us down the tunnel, the shadows reaching for our neck, and the sky was pink as if it was about to collide with the earth. We were on the brink of the abyss.

Are we still alive?

That world was vast and cold and only Dawn was there for comfort. We washed our red eyes in the river. All the birds were silent. There were only rocks and darkness, and the mountains in the distance, Memory and Loss. What gods lie here?

We picked a small rock against the wolves, when they come. We knew they would. They will eat our flesh when the world ends.

Where is home?

There's a hole in the wall with bushes outside and the sound of a piano. This whole strange land is at the tip of our fingers, until sometimes the room flies up in the air. If we'll get too close to the sun it may melt the roofing tiles. There are clean sheets on the bed and we lie beside Dawn. We listen to her breathe, watch the hair on her face. Peaceful. She doesn't notice us. And outside the wind caresses the windowpanes and everything is swirling gently. Silent clouds on a summer breeze. Ruins of time. Shreds of it floating in the air.

Her chest shivers.

As the sheets were stained with blood, there was nothing we could do. Old scars reopened. It's her period, holy blood. The clouds are watching beneath us. All is floating. All is leaking. It's time to go. We open the window to the clouds and let the wind take us, and as we breathe her eyes are opened wide.

Dawn's fingers on our cheeks.

We weren't there at all.

CHAPTER V

SHE AND Y

She wasn't very pretty and she was wearing a white shirt, and her hair was smooth, long, bright purple, and she was sixteen. She needed a place to sleep in Tel Aviv so we offered, and She came in. Now there was a new creature in our cave. She lay on her back in the dark, She insisted on the dark, and we crawled through it. Blackness was thick and her pussy was young, tight, freedom.

You can do it with your eyes closed.

The place was too hot for her and She couldn't sleep, and so She left to wander the night somewhere and may became a constellation in the night sky. We let her out, enjoyed our freedom, darkness slowly sucking our cock.

Wouldn't you go for it?

And when the night was over we wrote of all the people that were lost in the city, looking for the ocean, an escape. Through drugs, through drinks, through sex, whatever. Through Words. Through Love.

Y came at night and we held her.

"Are you okay?" We said.

"Yes. Are you?"

We didn't answer that. We just noticed the look in her eyes. It was only disappointment. Y drank less than usual and she seemed very careful as we talked, her hands in her lap. Her voice was quiet as she told us about her day.

Since it was summer vacation, she could go anywhere. She visited Pink and Lucas, and now us. We said nothing of Alice, even though something wanted us to. Y didn't mention her, and we figured she knows it's a misunderstanding. After all, pay attention now, she knew we were kind to her, and that we cared. She knew we were vicious too.

Her eyes told us that.

"What are you gonna do?" Said Y.

"I'm... I don't know yet. I'll be out of here in two weeks."

"And then what?"

Hot outside. We should have already finished or published our complete book, but instead we were just writing weird scenes and dreams, and Y. Then again, we didn't have much of a plan about what to do after that. We figured we'd be in our own world, eternal.

We could have ended up there that night, at her parents'. But the spirits left and Death just left us here. The whole thing...

"There are still some things I need to do."

"Like what?" Said Y, and her voice got pale.

"Just... in Europe." We said. "I need to finish something."

"And then what?" Her voice was almost a whisper.

"Finish something." We said.

We got up and started changing to our pajamas.

"You always do what you want." Said Y.

We looked at her. Why not?

"Doesn't it matter to you at all?" Said Y.

She bit her lip as we turned to face her.

"There are some things I have to do." We said. "And I can't always tell you why."

"Can you at least sometimes tell me?"

We got completely dressed and pushed her backward on the bed, until her back touched the wall. Then we took off her shoes and pulled her legs to flatten her body on the mattress. She was wearing a striped, white and yellow tank top. We turned off the light and soft darkness spread its fingers. The mirror was showing blurry figures, reflections of the moonlight through the closed window. We lay beside her.

"I know I can't control you and I'm not trying to." Said Y.

We didn't drink enough. Now there was no food in the cell, so we had to ration the liquid bread. She lay on her side facing us and we looked at her face. We've never seen her eyes so sad.

We smiled. She really was a lost child, and unfortunately for her, she found us at a very strange time of our life. We could have asked her about Lucas or about her ex, who's our age in case you forgot, but we didn't say a word. We let her try and make sense in a world, that she realized, to her horror, she was not yet ready for.

Something was scratching at the walls.

"I know there was Alice." Said Y with a shaky voice. "And I guess there were others too."

Smart, isn't she?

Why are you away from home, little girl, wandering the city at night with grown men?

What do you expect a beast to do when it comes upon a prey?

And you, say, what do you expect a beast to be, if not itself?

"So... you can do whatever you want. Really." She said.

She was lying. Trust us, we checked.

"Just tell me when you do it." Said Y.

"Yesterday." We smiled.

This was our lowest point.

Her wet eyes were now tearing. She closed them tightly and swallowed a silent wail. We were so strong we could crush her, and we showed her that. She'll never come back to us, and she'll be free of us. She'll be able to fly away.

But in the morning she was there, and we didn't know why.

It was sunny and we looked at her through tired eyes. At night we were far away, and now we looked at her back until she turned towards us. Red cheeks. Exhausted eyes. None of us smiled now, and none of us cried too.

You wonder why we don't explain ourselves. Well, we would have. But we have no idea what went on inside of us. We are many, and we are full of currents pushing in opposite directions. We had to do it. You have to believe us, we just had to.

Y was everything she should have been for us. We'll never forget that. However, we couldn't resist the urge, the mission. And Death sat up in bed behind here, over her, looking at us, and our thoughts were in his hand. He was waiting for our call.

But instead, we wrapped our arms around her and kissed her cheek lightly, and closed our eyes so we won't have to see this world and what we've done to it. Words can bring eternal life, and words can bring forth Death.

The morning was a flutter of dreams on eyelids, appearing, disappearing, reappearing. We moved between this world and others, and we saw empty rooms and evil men. Everyone was after us. But her breath was a reminder of something else. And our hold around her tightened, and we stayed there forever until her arms reached us. We felt them on our ribs, on our back, on our shoulders. But her eyes were closed.

There was a piano somewhere, and it took us far away. We never wanted to remember any of this. But our mission left us no choice. We turned and tossed in bed and didn't want to leave. This year was supposed to be a beginning, and it felt more and more like an end.

Then something moved and there was the room again, and we heard water touching the naked body of a child, hidden behind a wall. There was a cockroach on the wall but we couldn't move. It stood there, moving its antennae, staring at us.

It stared and stared, its eyes endless. Waiting for us to recognize him. And we did.

We were that roach.

Whose body is on the narrow bed?

Is he human?

And when we sat up the cell was empty. We opened the window and listened to the wind in the trees, and knew it is a warm day. We got in the shower and let it wash the nightmares and visions away.

We couldn't turn back time.

The door was opened and we bent over the toilet and looked out. Y locked the door behind her, tilted her head at us, and said:

"I went for a walk."

"With whom?" We said.

"Just me."

"Why did you come back?" We said.

"You should finish your shower."

We went back in the water and let it run. Let the hot water peel our skin off, help us shed it, then let the cold drops stop our blood. Only when we were shaking we got out and covered ourselves with a towel.

Y was reading our copy of "On the Road" by Jack Kerouac. Her legs were on the bed, one leg on the other, and her face was hidden. But we saw her head moving from side to side, as if she's hearing music.

It was all a dream.

Why would she be so at ease? So at home?

We got dressed and sat on the bed. We destroyed everything we could in this relationship, or whatever you want to call it. It was clear to us then and it's clear to us now.

"How was your sleep?" We said and sat on the bed.

Y put down the book. "It was good." She lied.

She put her legs on the floor and we got a little closer. Then we sat next to her, but our hands wouldn't touch her. She wasn't real, it was a phantasm made of dust particles in the air, shining in the rays of light that barely penetrated the cell from outside.

"Did you sleep well?" Said Y.

"I never sleep well." We said and got up and looked in the mirror.

Red eyes looked at us from there. Then Y got up too.

"I was thinking..." She said.

Now she's leaving. She just waited for us to wake up, so it would hurt us more.

"Maybe..." Y looked at the floor.

She has to leave. Can't she see she has to leave?

"Maybe..." Y looked at us and her eyes were wet again. "I was thinking."

She's not leaving.

She took our hands in hers. Tears wallowed in her brown, small eyes, under her blond curls glowing in the light of that summer day.

"Can we just..." Said Y. "Can we just... go see a movie? Please? Like... a normal couple?"

We all want normal. Is Love such a thing?

"Please?" She was sobbing. "Can we just..."

"Yes." We told Death, who was listening to every word. "Yes, we can."

She was sniffing harder and harder. She was shaking. We hugged her and we didn't let go.

"We can go now." Said this little girl in our arms.

"Yes." We sighed. "We can go now."

Death opened the door for us and we got out to the sunny street. It was close to noon and the sun was melting the trees and the people and the lamplights. There were puddles of people all over the road, boiling like water. And we walked along the main street towards the mall, and we held hands and said nothing.

And so it should always be.

And when we got inside the mall we found out that the theater's closed, but there was another one, and so we went there. We got out of the mall and turned to the street crossing it, and walked among the cafés. Moving away from the spice shop, from The Blue

Bar, from everything. The street was wide and all was open, and we could breathe.

Over the road arched a square and the sidewalks climbed to it from all directions, towards the sky, and the way took us there. The square over the road was full of pigeons. In the center was a colorful fountain, and Y seemed calm, if not happy.

She was still wearing her striped tank top and it matched her hair, which shone gold in the summer. It wasn't long. It only reached her shoulder blades. It was a waterfall of flame and we slid our hand on it, just to feel the silky waves.

Y looked.

Our hand was traveling from her curls to her shoulder, bare under the yellow strap, but warm. Wherever we touched our fingers left gentle, red, round markings on her skin. Her collarbone led us to her neck, and we felt her swallowing.

We never touched her in public.

We touched Moon, Pink, Alice, but never her.

Her neck was short and her chin was a little plump. And she held her mouth closed tightly, maybe so that we wouldn't kiss her, or so that her words won't come out.

There were words we couldn't say.

And so we let our hand follow her facial features to her lips, to her small nose and to her red cheeks. Her eyes were small and dark as half-moons. We could look inside them forever.

She swallowed again and bit her lip.

We just let our hand study her. The bridge of her nose and her dark eyebrows, and around her eyes. We could almost take one as a souvenir. Her round forehead, and her hair again. We let our hand memorize her in case she was lost. More lost than then, on the high square with us, close to the sky.

She came back the other night and she came back that morning. But her eyes said she won't stay for long. We won't either. We touched her cheek, and Death smiled.

Everything passes. Friends and women come into your life and walk away, just like water grazing the rocks of the banks. We can't hold them there. They slip through our fingers and continue to the sea. We can only bring our hand to our mouth and let our lips touch the wetness on our skin. That's all we can do. You too. You can't do any more than that.

But we can write them. We can make them real once more, as visions, as voices. Make them stay a little while longer, read them off the page, and store it for safekeeping. So Y will always be with us, whether she likes it or not.

The difference would be, she won't even realize that.

But maybe she realized, as we went inside the theater for a matinee, where darkness shrouded the outside and the theater was almost empty. We watched the dreams on the big screen and when it went dark we just kept sitting there.

"Aren't you coming?" Said Y.

"I like staying." We said. "Let everyone flood the exits. What's the rush?"

And so we and Y sat there in the empty theater, on black leather chairs, watching the screen. There was nothing on it. The light was pale yellow. And when everyone was out, we walked out too.

Were we normal then?

If that really happened...

Were we normal, sitting in the dark, our hands touching, watching other worlds on a screen? Surrounded by people, by the whole human safari...

Is that normal to you?

Holding a girl's hand in the theater, feeling her warmth? Skin on skin, pulse on pulse. Knowing she's there to see it with you. Is that normal?

"Thank you." Said Y outside.

"Where are you going?" We said.

"I'll be with my parents for a while." She said. "My birthday's next month. You should come. Everyone's coming. Lucas too. You could... talk about writing."

"It'll be okay. I'll come for you." We said with our hand on her head.

Finally, after going through hell, Y smiled.

ON THE ROOF

CHAPTER I

~

GO BACK TO THE BEGINNING

We're being left in bus stations all the time, stranded, to continue our life with a missing part. And so it was time to accept this, and let all the girls pass, and give up the roach infested room and find something else. Only, we didn't have money for something else.

As we came back from the hotel one sunny day, we stopped outside a small restaurant we used to frequent many times before. We counted the small change in our hand.

We were missing one coin to buy something to eat.

We went back to the room for a meal of baked beans with tomato sauce. We had one can left. And that's when Puff called.

"Are you okay?" We said.

"I dunno. Are you?"

Her voice sounded as if it's coming from far away. From another world maybe.

"I don't know." We said. "I heard you left the shop."

"Yeah. I'm done with it."

Aren't we all?

"I'm done with this city."

"Tell me about it."

We got up to look at the mirror. There was something there.

"Remember how we talked about acid? I told you I'll never touch it." She said. "I told you I'm too scared."

We put our fingertips to the mirror wall. It was there, blocking us from passing through.

For now.

"Well, so I did it. I went to this rave a few weeks ago. And I just did it."

"How did it feel?"

"I saw things... I felt them..."

We turned away from the mirror and looked out the window. The windowpanes were only half open, as the cell was too small for them to open fully.

"I can't say what. Don't ask me. It's very... private... when you do something like that."

"Where are you now?"

The bushes outside were solid as rocks. There were no birds this day, but we could hear the cars in the street. Everyone's on their feet in this city, all the time.

"Up north. I can't go back to the city."

"The northern part? You're not too far from me."

"No, no." She said. "Way north. I found a little place here, on the mountain, away from Tel Aviv. Away from any city."

For a moment, we wished we could do the same. We had no need for this city anymore.

Our ritual was a failure.

Everything was.

"It's so peaceful... quiet. I can hear God talking to me."

"Oh." Said we. "What is he saying?"

"Don't make fun of it. I've experienced such beautiful things."

Well, one less girl to fuck.

But she was right.

We were in the belly of the city, and we came out bare and forsaken.

We should have known better.

You should have, too.

"What about you?" Said Puff.

"I'm planning my leaving." We said.

"Be careful."

"Of what?"

"I dunno." Said Puff. "It's... a gut feeling."

And that was all.

We've known Puff for a short period of time, and she was a counselor and a guide to us. We could talk to her about the spirits. We didn't want her to be far away when we are stuck in the city. But we didn't have much of a choice, now, did we?

We were left alone with ourselves, and we had no choice but to keep writing, and keep going. Death was in the room too and he took out some blood from our legs, but he was waiting patiently and we knew we have to complete our mission.

It wasn't up to us.

Summer brought with it the end of our stay in our hole in the wall, and we decided to not renew our contract. We left the hotel too, so we had all the time in the world. We could do anything.

Where would we go?

The bookstore at the mall was an option. What can we find in those books there?

We wondered about it. So we walked, but we never got there. Neither will you.

Come with us, this one last time.

Because in our cell, the roaches will crawl out of their holes to gnaw at the drywall. They will eat the bed, the chair, the toilet... all will be gone.

We also didn't hear from Y for about a month, and we didn't know what we could say.

We could say she's really young and we have no future together. We could also say it was nice having her over so she can suck our cock and we can touch her breasts. We could also say she's not really our type, and so it's not like it's love from first sight...

But then again, we couldn't say it.

We cared too much.

We lay on a bench on the main boulevard under the trees, and let them cast shapes on our face. The wind rattled them, and the light spots on our face moved like waves. We were very tired of the past month, which stretched over ages.

We don't know if we fell asleep there, with our bag of notebooks, but our eyes were opened and we sat up. It always comes when you least expect it, and when the situation is the least comfortable.

But we had no other choice.

A world was lost, and a world was being built.

Green wind started blowing around us as we wrote and the leaves were fireflies. One landed on our page and we moved it quickly and kept smearing ink on the paper. We didn't see or know anything from this world anymore. We were treading a new bridge that we were building, and sometimes we were walking so fast we were walking on air.

On the other end of the bridge we were out of this body, free to mold our own world. We were floating in the Nothing that was left after the Everything. We were the tip of a pencil on the floor of a dark, empty theater. The ticking of a clock. Or the footsteps of ants.

Words form life.

We looked at the ant on the tip of our finger. Then we blew on it, and the creature was riding on the wind. Our pinky was blue with ink.

We should do this with blood.

When we raised our head we saw another writing on the wall.

Looking straight at us.

Step by step, we crossed the road towards it.

Writers N.ever Die.

And we just knew it. It's him again. N. It was written in black, underlined, and the letters were leaning to our right.

To our right, there was a newspaper on another bench. We crouched and unfolded it and looked at the headline, but it was nothing unusual. Our eyes skimmed the page.

Y are you here? N.

The wind blew in our hair.

We got up, still holding it, and got back to our own bench. All of those inscriptions came from the same source. The city was full of them, but nobody noticed but us. Well, no wonder. They were meant for us. We found nothing else in the paper.

Why are we here?

N knows Y.

N said, Look for no. 14.

Her age.

Then he said, C-U.G.

And our legs took us there. The sun was beginning to set and it was Thursday, which means the place should be open. However, it wasn't, and the sign just said, We're sorry to inform that we moved. Tonight.

We knocked anyway, just to see if there's someone there. Even the cleaning lady. We didn't care. We looked around for goths and other people that might be associated, but saw no such people. They had to write a new address, didn't they? Otherwise, how could people find them? There has to be a phone number or a secret code. Maybe there was.

We looked at the sign again and noticed something we haven't noticed before. It was black letters printed on white.

We're sorry to iN.form that we moved. toN.ight. EterN.al life is N.igh.

Oh.

The things you can find...

But we still didn't know where it was. Who the fuck is N, and how come he knows Y?

How come we know Y? Well, she heard about us from someone. And she likes the creative types, too, like Pink and Lucas and us. It only made us think of her. We didn't know where she was, whether she's with Lucas or not, and we tried to decide if we should call her.

Lucas was named Night on her phone. It was his online nickname.

Our legs started walking even before we realized where to. We were supposed to go to the bookstore, but we forgot all about it. More like, it was in the back of our mind, but we didn't mind it staying there.

We have to say "yes".

Luckily, as you know, we are never alone. So we let our legs lead while the answer came to us.

Y liked older writers. Her ex was also one. Believe us. Just like Lucas, Night.

The sky grew darker as we walked, searching for his building. There were no clouds, but no stars or moon either. There was only a sheet of black cloth over the city, covering everything like a swamp. Soon will come The Worm again.

We were walking south the whole time. On one stone wall there was another graffiti.

Go back to the beginning. N.

Does he mean our first encounter, when we were near his home? Is that the beginning?

This was his neighborhood, where we previously walked with him. Where we walked with Pink, who kind of asked us to rape her. Our pleasure, lady. Then she left us and we continued with Lucas, and there was a writing on the wall, Write like you mean it, and Lucas saw it. It was signed by N.

Lucas could see it.

Oh, yeah.

The streets were getting narrower and orange light took control of the night. This is where Pink and Lucas were, where Y spent a lot of her nights, and where we found a fetish club to dance in. People were walking around in groups, all the whores and dealers, all the migrants and dumpster diving vegans. The entire human safari, its hidden parts.

A big, ugly fish looked at us from behind a display window. The sign taped to the aquarium read:

Y was here. N.

We picked one street and followed it. We don't really know why.

Sometimes, in dreams, you do things that seem unreasonable. Like you have no good reason, or you should even do the opposite. But you do them anyway. We didn't even count our fingers. We didn't care. What does it matter?

All you need is writing. It can grant you anything you lack and take you anywhere you want. It can conjure up all the girls and all the stars, and make snakes into dragons. It can form eternal life.

We stopped next to Pink's building. The buildings in this area were a little taller. Y could be there, hiding from... from someone. Lucas could also be there. Maybe it was all a surprise party and we were just about to ruin it. A sign at the entrance to a small grove said:

Look up. N.

The building was tall and we decided to go there. If we won't find Lucas, at least we'll find Pink. Then we could make good on that promise. The path slithered between the trees, and we climbed up to the dark entrance. It was locked and we didn't know the code to the intercom.

163

We checked the names on the mailboxes by the doors. Most of the name tags were empty, some were just names. On the name tag of the last apartment were four digits and a letter.

1415. N.

Last floor. No elevator. We climbed up the stairs and listened to all the screeches and all the little noises you only hear at nights. Like the things scratching the walls from the inside. The light didn't work and our bag was a little heavy. As we were climbing to the fourth floor we saw an inscription on the wall. It was framed in a square of orange light that entered the stairwell through a small, round, glassless window. Just a hole in the wall.

She hates you.

It was probably true.

We got to the floor and on the electric panel was another inscription.

You failed.

It was absolutely true.

We were exhausted from this city.

On the wall, there was another inscription.

We will kill you.

This can be true, too.

There was no one there but Death, and he was an old and welcomed friend. And dying can increase the sales of any art form, including books. We climbed and saw another inscription.

Stay with us.

Then another.

You are already dead.

We reached the fifth floor. Red letters were smeared on one of the doors.

Go back to the beginning.

Now we knew what it was. The beginning, before we got here, our comfort zone. Sitting at home with our computer, reading, talking to no one. Cutting wrists. Chatting with Death.

Go back to the beginning.

Back in time to before we landed here and killed ourselves with lust. Before we went on stage half naked and lost friends and alienated people. Before we messed around with all those lousy girls, and lost the only one who was actually good to us.

Go back to the beginning.

Home. Home. The comfort of the bed and of our small town, to solitude. When our body was ours and we were alone, when all we wanted was a decent job and someone to call "girlfriend". No fame, no glory, no eternal life.

The place where there were never whiskey or beer.

Night, or Lucas, was playing games. But he was right.

When we arrived in Tel Aviv, the big city, we carried a backpack of dreams. Our arrival didn't go as planned, though, and we were left with a hole in the wall and with a fourteen year old Goldilocks. We wanted to get out of our shell and live, and we let other forces possess us.

Now we had no money, no job, no place to sleep, no Y.

At the top of the stairs was a door, with letters smeared on it. We climbed towards it in the dark.

What goes up must come down.

And we opened the door and stepped outside to the roof.

CHAPTER II

~

ON THE ROOF

It was all of us up there. We saw Lucas, and we saw Death. Lucas's pale eyes looked straight at us. He looked as if he was rehearsing this forever, and now his prey has finally arrived. But he looked terrified, too. The night was starless, black, a sheet of leather. If you followed everything up until that moment, you know it shouldn't have ended that way. But that summer we felt like drowning in air.

We were done.

"You should have given up long ago." Said Lucas.

We put down our backpack filled with secret notebooks and incantations, and hid our hands in our pockets. Then we noticed the inscriptions.

The roof was full of words, smeared in black and red graffiti. We couldn't make sense of it, but every now and then a word leaped into our line of sight.

Beginning

Eternal

Kill

Our own words got locked in our throat. We were so tired we could barely think. We didn't even know why we were there.

Did we fail?

Did he succeed?

The words came in and out of our line of sight like they were dancing to the beat of the wind. It was kind of disorienting, and we almost lost sight of the pale man on the roof.

Lucas, or should we say Night, stood there slouching. His pale blond hair was wild like a lightning storm, and his hands were shaking.

"Who are you?" We said.

"Who are you?" Said Night. "Why are you here?"

Who called us to this city? We looked at Death, and he calmed us down with a simple gesture of his hand. It was almost time.

"Yes, I'm talking to you! Don't look away!" Said Night. "Who do you think you are?"

Well, he was mad.

"We," our lips said. "Are many."

Night's jaw dropped. He didn't have to talk, anyway. His words were all around us, berating us for Y and for our writing. We weren't dedicated enough to any of them. And his words reminded us of that.

You couldn't ever write. Said one inscription.

You shouldn't have come. Said another.

We will kill you.

Then we noticed this little sound, drops hitting the concrete roof.

Tap.

Tap.

Tap.

And we looked at our hands, dripping bright red.

"You shouldn't have come." Said Night. "And you shouldn't have touched her."

"She touched us." We said.

"Why?" Said Night. "Why you? Why does she like you so much? Why does everyone like you so much? How come you can do all those things?"

We were doing what we wanted to do, since the moment we arrived. We didn't have to tell him this. He knew. Somehow, he knew. But he was rambling in his madness.

"How come she chose you? And why I am the one that has to come second, or last? You can't even write. You never could. You shouldn't have come here. You're lazy, sloppy, you can't write a thing. You'll never accomplish anything, and nothing will be left of you!"

It was all true, maybe.

And as we looked at our palm, we saw the blood that pooled in the creases of our flesh. All of our old wounds were open now.

When you cut into the present, the future leaks out.

Our forearm was covered with bleeding cuts, shining red in the starless darkness. There was no orange light coming from the streets like a sun burning. We didn't even notice it was gone, but then we took a step towards the edge and saw nothing in the abyss. Death was looking too.

Where has the street gone?

Or are we just too tired?

"When you write you make the moment eternal." Said Night. "People are wrong when they think writing is all about imagining stuff. It never is."

Write like you mean it.

It's about keeping our stories safe. It's about taking temporary humans and making them eternal. All the people are filled with stories, private stories, embarrassing ones. Stories of failures and broken heart, of mishaps and deep intimacy. Writing is conserving a human alive, even after his body is gone.

We knew all that.

Apparently, Night also knew about it.

"You can't write." He said. "Even Y said that. You can only scribble in your notebooks. You should quit now, you can't do it. At first they wanted me to put an eye on you, because maybe you have it in you. But not only you can't create a world, you can't even manage your own. All you do is fill those notebooks with unreadable sentences that make no sense, and all you can write is what you steal from your favorite authors. You should be a reader. It's good for you. You can't create anything."

All those words were swirling around us in black and white, like a huge chess board, and we were the tip of a pencil on it. Trying to leave our mark. Words in black and red.

Red as blood.

Blood.

Bright red.

When you cut into the present, the future leaks out.

Our pants were stained with it, as the cuts on our legs opened too. Our forearms and the back of our palms were dripping on our cloths and on the concrete roof. We looked at the persistent stain of ink on our little finger, the one that marked us as writers after each session of scribbling and scribbling over the pages. The ink on our finger was now covered in blood.

We were bleeding our body away.

When we looked down we had no feet. There was only concrete and the words inscribed on it.

Eternal life is nigh.

Night was so near we could feel him. Whether we were the ones approaching him or he was the one approaching us, we did not know. Our body was formless, shapeless, like blood. Blood mixed with ink.

Writing in blood.

Our blood is acid.

We pushed our palm to Night's face and he stumbled backwards. He tried to wipe it off. But our blood was a coded inscription.

We crouched and drew a circular line with our blood and surrounded ourselves with our own flesh made ink.

Night turned pale, and Death smiled.

"Why did she choose you?" He screamed.

His face was disfigured. He was hunching, his hands were now shaking so hard he could barely close them, and his knees bent. Our blood was dripping down from his forehead and eyes, filling his acne scars, dripping down his lips and chin. He was a disaster.

He was also weak. A person maddened by hate, mumbling incoherently about how ugly and unloved he is, while we are too popular everywhere we go. We had no choice but to sit there cross legged and look at his panic attack takes control of him. We never hated anyone. Not those girls, not the waiters, not anyone else... they were all a story to tell. Y was a story to tell.

Night was mad with hate.

We were mad with love.

We loved life. We loved everything they could offer. We loved all that's hidden in the night and at the bottoms of beer bottles. We loved raging through this world with no fear, doing what we want, however we want, and whenever we want. With no Fear or Hatred we had no masters, and we were free to roam the streets and minds of others, and our own.

We loved Y. Oh, we loved her so. We loved her with every bone and with every drop of blood. And our blood was full of it. We only wished we could tell her so. And as Night fell on his knees, our blood burning his face even more and his tears are running, we noticed all the words inside our circle.

We were writing everything that came to our mind all the time.

We loved Y. Oh, we loved her so. We loved her with every bone and with every drop of blood.

Our head was light from lack of blood. Our hands were trembling. We didn't feel our body and it was time for us to leave.

We are King.

Our words were our power. The bloody words that spread around us were a counter-spell, a mark we left on time. Now we didn't have to eat nor drink, fuck nor sleep, talk nor breathe. And if Night didn't stare at us that way, we could have just left it at that.

But his eyes were murderous and he was serious about killing us. He started swaying towards our circle, but we leaned forward and wrote another passage outside it, right next to the bloody, red line.

And as our shaky finger wrote, Death grew happier. His smile grew wider with each and every letter. Finally. He was so patient.

"Can you read upside down?" We said.

Right over the words spelling We are King, three more words were now inscribed on this world forever.

We bring Death.

And Death was tall and mighty behind us, and as he bent forward towards Night, who was standing outside the circle hunching, Death peeled off his own nose and let Night stare into it.

Night lifted his eyes.

He was white, and a light stain spread on his pants.

Instead of a nose, there was a black hole in Death's face. And as you looked inside you could notice the sparks of red and orange. Flowery embers. There were rivers of fire burning inside Death's body, and Night fell back.

Death was towering above him.

And he swooped down and swallowed Night whole.

Then Death straightened his back and our back straightened. He dropped his hands and our hands dropped. He was filled with fire, we were filled with air.

And then he held our shoulders.

We are King.

We bring Death.

CHAPTER III

❧

AMETHYST WINGS

Go back to the beginning.

I sit in my cell staring at the butterflies floating in the hall. As light as if they were never there. Hovering like stars with wings of neon purple and phosphoric green. Electric butterflies freely playing outside and laughing at me in colors.

I'm waiting for a long time now. It could be ages. Only me and those walls and the nothingness that's beyond them. I only know there are big, brown eyes floating in space looking at me all the time. Those butterflies are nothing but the slivers of the tight pupils. They await me outside.

It's not my fault. I just couldn't help myself. And as I collapsed my only choice was to turn my soul in. I closed my eyes and floated through space.

Now I am here.

After slithering through moist tunnels I was able to find this cell and rest in it. Watch the butterflies. I used to eat butterflies once, before I shed my skin and killed and escaped.

Escaped from where? From what?

I can't tell. The butterflies are silent as they approach. They gather around my forearms but they can't find any blood.

I am a vacuum.

173

The butterflies sit, resting. I don't move. I only wait. Soon, I know, this too shall pass. And so I lean against the wall and I don't feel it, but the butterflies turn into white fingers. I know it's her. But now, for now, I am protected. These are my walls, and here I wait. All I can see is reflections on the butterflies' wings. They show figures, but they're too blurry to recognize. They show endless streets. They show me all of eternity in a piece of paper. Everything that happened, happens, and will happen, over and over again, time after time after time. And it's all the same.

When you cut into the present, the future leaks out.

All is a mirror. It will all repeat itself forever. Nothing new is in existence. This is why I am here. We float in the Nothing that remained after the Everything. There are no boundaries outside.

What do dying dreams leave in their wake?

I know there are big, brown eyes floating in space looking at me all the time. The butterflies flutter and leave and I know it is time.

Loss and Memory, they're here to stay.

I am never alone.

I am on my knees.

Forehead touching the cold stone.

Everything is laughing.

And here they are in front of me.

Now I walk through the bloody hall. Loss on one side and his teeth are crooked beneath his swine nose. Memory on the other side and his eyes are full of ancient wisdom that they are not supposed to possess. There's nothing in front of me and the shadows are gone too.

Were there others before?

In this place?

Or is it mine alone?

I walk the hall for ages. In the distance I see a ball of light. The sun of another brain who's still alive somewhere, clear, and he'll be here when he's ready. Everyone gets here in the end. Deep inside the dark side of their soul, where the mind no longer shines.

My eyes are dripping. I am blissful.

Electricity runs through every cell of my body and I feel the discharge. She's calling me with an echo that never fades. Ready to swallow me with a worm tongue.

Loss and Memory let me go and I fall. Every pair of stars is a pair of eyes, and they're all watching as I fall. I stretch my hands and all is far away. I can't grab anything. Just forever fall into her eyes.

I see beneath me an orange ball of light. I am dwarfed by it a thousand times.

Go back to the beginning.

I now have scales again, but they are not the same. They are silver, and my fall becomes a soft glide towards the light. I'm floating down on amethyst wings, my body no longer crawls.

The orange light awaits me.

I'm a tip of a pencil on the floor of a dark, empty theater.

The ticking of a clock. Or the footsteps of ants. The squeal of a door going back and forth.

CHAPTER IV

～

AWAY FROM YOU

The porch is full of people. The house too. I'm already starting to regret this birthday party. But I'm worrying too much. I should let them all entertain themselves. They're grown-ups, after all.

He didn't come.

I let him know it's today and still he didn't come. Neither of them, actually. But why do I need such people in my life anyway? I never get what I deserve.

I should stop all this.

"A drink?" Says Joseph.

He was with me that night, at my parents' house, when we carried him up the stairs. Joseph's glasses are glittering in the night.

"No." I say. "I quit."

"Completely?"

"Yeah." I let out a chuckle.

He comes and sits next to me. "What's wrong?"

"I'm not a party person."

"Hm." He says. "With no music and no food, I'm not sure that this even qualifies as a party."

Now I laugh. He's right, though. What can I do? Even my friends are not party people. I don't think any of them has ever been to a club. Well, besides him. But it was a different kind of club.

All my friends were artists and writers and musicians, and they're all twenty something and have their own problems. I wanted to be like that too. I wanted to be a writer or an actress or do anything artsy. It seemed fun, but it's not, really. It demands a lot of people if they take it seriously.

I used to have friends who took it very seriously.

I haven't heard from any of them in the past month. But that's a good thing, isn't it?

"What is?" Says Joseph.

"Oh, did I say that out loud?"

"You just said it's a good thing." Joseph barely looks at me. "Are you thinking about him?"

"About who?"

He shrugs. "Lucas or..."

"No. Not at all." I lie.

"It's for the best, probably." Says Joseph. "None of them should come."

I think about it. He's right. But still...

"You're angrier than I am." I say.

"I really am." He says. "All writers are mad."

I can't answer that. I chose this path, and now I had to choose another. That was the only reasonable thing that I could find. I can't complain for jumping in the cage with leopards. But I can't answer and I remain busy with my thoughts until people start leaving. There are trillions of stars outside.

Everybody came but him.

"Oh." I hear a voice as someone opens the door.

Joseph gets ups to check. Then the door closes and he says, "How are you?"

"Where is she?"

I swallow. Joseph is too polite. He shouldn't let people he doesn't like inside his apartment. But he does, and the footsteps are getting closer. I notice I'm wringing my fingers in my lap.

But I'm okay.

I hope.

A tall shadow enters the porch and he comes in right after it. I haven't seen him in a month, his hair is long and dark and wavy. His face is thin, his lips are big and his eyes are dark too. I spent so much time looking into them.

"How are you?" He says.

I get up to give him a hug, but he barely returns one. He puts one hand on my head and lets go. Then he offers an open beer bottle.

"Do you want to help me finish this?"

"I don't drink anymore." I say. "I decided to quit."

"Oh." He says. "Too bad."

Joseph is right. Some people never learn.

We sit together on the couch and Joseph appears.

"Is everything okay?" He says.

"Yeah. We're just talking." I tell him. And myself as well.

"Happy birthday." He says after Joseph disappears. "You're fifteen."

"Yeah."

"How is it?"

"It's nice." I try not to smile. "It's okay."

"Nothing's changed." He says, not even looking at me.

When he does, I don't know what to say.

"Are you going away?" I say.

"Where to?"

"I dunno. You said you have stuff to do."

"Oh." He says. "Europe. Yes. I'm going away."

"When will you be back?"

"I don't know. I'll tell you when I do." He says and takes a sip.

I want to tell him not to, but I just say, "Okay".

"What are your plans?" He says and puts the empty bottle on the floor.

He doesn't go to get another one.

"I'm gonna start attending a boarding school in Jerusalem."

"Wow." He says. "How come?"

"It'll get me out of the house." I hear myself say.

Away from here.

Away from you.

"I thought you wanted to be an actress."

"I changed my mind." I say. "And you? Are you still gonna be a writer?"

"There's nothing else I can do." He says.

The porch is silent, the stars are glowing. The night is deep purple. Only Joseph's in the house, both because it's his and also because he wants to watch over me. He's trying too hard.

"Do you want to take a walk outside?" He says.

"Not really."

"Okay."

179

We open our mouths at the same time, but he gives up and lets me continue.

"You look weird." I say. "What have you been through this past month?"

"I'm just... walking." He says.

"Where to?" I say.

"Back... to the beginning." He lowers his head.

"I don't understand."

He turns towards me and my body does the same. He's close and I can touch him, I could have, I used to want to. But it had to be in return of something, and I didn't get that something. I have to keep my distance.

He says my name.

"I write." He says. "I write all my thoughts, all my dreams, all my memories, all my feelings. That's what I do. That's what I know. In the past month... I left my room. I'm not there anymore. But when I read my notebooks the room is there, and you are there."

He waits to see if I interrupt. I don't. He doesn't say this as a pleading. His voice is dry and quiet as if he's giving a lecture. So he continues:

"My first notebook had a first page. And my last notebook has a last page. And all this city and all that has happened, is bordered between those two pages. This is my life, this is my book. And books have a beginning and an end, so I am destined to read those pages over and over again and look for clues in them, forever. This is... eternal life."

The world is still. Nothing moves. There is no wind, no birds, no cars. We only see the satellite dishes and the solar water heaters on the rooftops.

"What are you saying?" I say.

"My eyes see the past." He says and sighs. "And I will live it anew forever."

He gets up without saying a word and bends over the railing. I almost jump up to stop him from jumping, but he just turns around, says goodbye and walks back in.

Death leaves with him. He looks at me one last time before he disappears, tall and slender. Nostrils fuming. A witness to all that has happened. I nod at him and he walks away.

I hear him say goodbye to Joseph and the door opens and then closes.

"Are you okay?" Joseph appears in the porch.

I get up and hug him, and he hugs me tightly with both hands.

I'm finally alone.

Made in the USA
Monee, IL
01 March 2020

22560403R20105